I0628245

Sinamatella

A Quest for Meaning

Sinamatella

A Quest for Meaning

A Novel by

Shlomo Breznitz

 SAMUEL WACHTMAN'S SONS

 DEKEL PUBLISHING HOUSE

Sinamatella - A Quest for Meaning

Shlomo Breznitz

Copyright © 2014

Dekel Publishing House
www.dekelpublishing.com

North American rights by
Samuel Wachtman's Sons, Inc.
ISBN 978-1-888820-66-9

All rights reserved. No portion of this book, except for brief review, may be reproduced, stored in a retrieval system, or transmitted in any form or by any means – electronic, mechanical, photocopying, recording, or otherwise – without written permission of the publisher. For information regarding international rights please contact Dekel Publishing House, Israel; for North American rights please contact Samuel Wachtman's Sons, Inc., U.S.A.

Chief Editor:	Hugo N. Gerstl
Language Editing:	Kathleen Roman
Proof Reading:	Ruti Frankel

Cover image:
Savanna sunset, South Africa © Nico Smit, Dreamstime.com

Inside images:
Savannah landscape with animals © Luminita Lupu, Dreamstime.com

Cover design and typesetting by

For information contact:

Dekel Publishing House	**Samuel Wachtman's Sons, Inc.**
P.O. Box 45094	2460 Garden Road, Suite C
Tel Aviv 6145002, Israel	Monterey, CA 93940, U.S.A.
Tel: +972 3506-3235	Tel: 831 649-0669
Fax: +972 3506-7332	Fax: 831 649-8007
Email: info@dekelpublishing.com	Email: samuelwachtman@gmail.com

To Zvia

Tremor

In his office, fondling the clean, laser-printed sheets of his latest report, Don counts the pages once more. He knows that there are twelve pages in the main document, and twenty-six in the appendices, making thirty-eight in all, and the numbers are actually nicely printed in the top right corner of each page, with the exception of the title page, of course, but the temptation to count again is just too great. Each appendix is labeled with a letter, and has its own numbers, starting from one. The last appendix is the longest of the lot, and he wonders if for the sake of balance he shouldn't divide it in two. He likes the numbering system of his reports, and he likes the top right corner position. Some people center page numbers at the top, forcing readers to look at them first thing on turning the page. Don is convinced that this disrupts the fluency of reading a document, and constitutes a major error. Putting the number at the bottom of each page, or in the top left corner, produces the same effect. Only the top right corner allows readers to resume where they left off on the page before, perhaps without even noticing the number. He always notices the numbers and their positions, not only on his own reports, but on every document that passes through his hands.

*One…and two…and three…and four…*he needs a rather long *aaand* to allow time for the turning of the page and picking up the next one. The report is neatly stacked and it is difficult to pick up just one page at a time. He hesitates to put pressure on the corners, something that he knows helps, so as not to damage the clean sheets. On reaching six he cheats with the *and*, making it double its usual length, since six is such a short number to pronounce. *Six. Seven compensates for the six. Se-v-en. Ei-g-ht. Ni-ne. T-e-n.* He searches for the center of each word, a favorite thing of his. He likes long words that allow for division into groups of three letters at a time—first he counts the letters, then devises a strategy for locating the median. He believes the report is excellent. *Exc-ell-ent* makes nine, the symmetry prescribes four letters from each side, and the solution is *ex-ce-l-le-nt*. It is difficult when you have to divide double letters. They like to stick together.

He presses the intercom for his secretary. Dorothy, good old Dorothy, who has been with him from the very beginning, takes her time. "Yes, Mr. Mendelson?" Never Don.

"Dorothy, please prepare the cover letter to go with our report. It's ready now and should be sent today. And please bring me the other letters to sign."

"Yes, Mr. Mendelson, right away."

"Thanks, Dorothy."

He lets go of the intercom and straightens in his chair. His back hurts, and he needs to stretch properly, but cannot, since Dorothy might enter any moment now. There are no papers on his large desk besides the report. He moves it toward the edge of the table and gently blows twice to remove any dust that might have remained behind. He is now ready.

Come on, Dorothy, what's taking you so long? Come on, there is no time to waste. He taps the clean desk with the fingers of his right hand, getting into a rhythm. *Taaaaap tap tap. Taaaaap tap tap.* Finally the door opens and she enters, carrying the letters. Her hands appear to clutch the paper too tightly. She has old hands, and this morning when she brought in his coffee, he noticed a quiver, nothing serious, but a quiver just the same. He wonders when Dorothy plans to retire, and how he would manage without her. She knows most of his whims and peculiarities, and never gossips. Even Claire likes her, although lately she seems less patient with her.

"How can you stand it, she is getting stiffer by the day."

Typical Claire. *Typ-i-cal Cla-ire.*

He reads the letters while she stands waiting. Her face, barely visible above the page, distracts him. This is ridiculous. Why doesn't she leave him alone? Proofreading calls for all of one's attention. Lately he has found an occasional typo, and thinking her honor is at stake, she prefers to wait. He sees that she spelled *colour* with a *u* like the English do, but decides to overlook it. He reads on: "It is our opinion that all the relevant files should be sent to this office for inspection as soon as possible, and under no circumstances later than the end of this month..." In spite of himself he keeps going back to the sentence beginning with, "As you have noticed, the places where we would like to introduce a comment have been marked in a different *colour* for your convenience." The word glares at him from the page, unwilling to let go. After all, the *u* makes it six letters instead of five, completely shifting the median. Dorothy asks if there is a problem and he, hating himself for it, shows her. She picks up all of the letters, including the good ones that he hasn't signed yet, and leaves. It was a mean thing to do to her. The British spelling is quite acceptable and it carries with it an aura of learned seriousness. *I should actually spell it that way on purpose,* he muses. *It can only bring me respect.*

The phone rings and he lets it ring exactly three times before picking it up. He always does that, and he always picks up the phone very slowly. No need to rush. It is Claire, and the warmth of her "Hello, Don" is two on a scale of ten. Over the years he had learned to monitor her voice quite precisely and is rarely wrong. He responds to her voice almost automatically. "Hello Claire, what is the matter? Did something happen?"

A pause. She hesitates. "Yes, Don, I must speak with you… urgently."

His heart skips a beat. "What is it, Claire? Are you alright?"

Another pause. Unlike Claire. *Unl-ike Cla-ire.* "Yes, I'm alright, but I must speak with you urgently." She had said so already, using exactly the same works.

"What is it? Can't you tell me what the problem is?"

"No, Don. Not on the phone, please."

His heart skips two more beats. "So come, quickly."

"No, not in your office, please. Let's meet at the coffee shop across the street. In two minutes." She hangs the phone. He holds onto the receiver, unable to think clearly. Something is terribly wrong. Two minutes? That means she is actually calling from nearby. *Why? Why?*

Why not in my office? He puts the phone down very slowly, slower than usual. This has never happened before. An accident? The children? Her mother? Claire herself? When had she had her mammogram? And her pap smear? Could it be her mammogram? Now, that is a word. *Mammog-ram* makes nine, so it is four from each side, and the solution is *mamm-o-gram.*

He is on his way out. Dorothy looks up from her computer, but he doesn't see her. Out of the office and into the elevator in less than forty seconds. Thirty-seven to be exact. The damned elevator stops at almost every floor. He looks at his watch. Almost two minutes now. He measures the time it takes the elevator to negotiate a single stop. There are too many people in the elevator. He doesn't look at them, but feels the crowd. They are standing too close for comfort. Finally. He makes an effort not to rush and exits the elevator as if it was his lunch break. He feels slightly dizzy, and wonders what would happen were he to faint suddenly. Would someone recognize him? After working in this building for almost twelve years—it would be twelve on October 17—would someone recognize him? This is suddenly very important to him and stepping out of the elevator he searches the hall for familiar faces. *If someone looks familiar does it guarantee that I look familiar to him? Too complicated. I must think about this later, when this emergency is over.* For this is surely an *em-er-g-en-cy.*

When he enters the coffee shop she is already there. He sees her immediately. It is difficult not to see Claire immediately. She looks very pale. Don gives her the perfunctory kiss first on her left cheek and then on her right. She seems to be undecided about whether to stand up or keep on sitting. The greeting over, he takes his seat and faces her.

He decides not to push her. Now that fate seems to be calling, he wants to maintain a measure of dignity. Another "What happened?

Are you OK?" would not do. Suddenly Don, for the first time in more than three minutes, feels oddly calm. He studies her face, and by the time she speaks he can almost sense what is coming.

"It is over between us, Don. We cannot go on like this."

During the pause between her words he is struck by the *cannot*, which replaced her usual *can't*. It is so British sounding, almost like colour and honour. And amour. No moure.

"I am leaving today. Please try to understand. It is over."

Don wonders what's over. Why? With whom? For there must be someone else, right? Still, he remains quiet. Stubbornly quiet. He looks at her. Who is she? Where did she come from? Where is she going? Why? Oh, Why?

"Why?" he cries. "What happened? Are you OK? What is over? Why? Is there someone else?" Suddenly everything came out and he is unable to stop it. "Claire, please!" Dignity or not, there is nothing he can do about it anymore.

She starts crying, her beautiful dark eyes suddenly wet, her face contorted. He hunts for a tissue. "Please, Don, don't make a scene. It's no use. Please, let's part as friends."

He feels his anger mounting, coming up all the way from his chest. He will burst open soon. First faint in the elevator, then burst open in the coffee shop. *What is happening to me? What did I do to deserve this? And where have I been while this was brewing? Why didn't I know about it? And where has her love suddenly gone? Suddenly? Sud-de-nly? Oh, damn the word!* His anger takes a strange turn, focusing on the word *suddenly*. It is a frightening word and he hates it.

"Why so suddenly?" he asks.

And before he can stop her, oddly aware of what the answer might be and afraid to hear it, her face in better control now, she whispers, "It's not sudden, Don. It has been long in the making…very long." And thinking that this is perhaps the best timing for the final act, she leaves.

Don makes no effort to follow her, and clutching the tissue that he was too slow to offer her, he gazes at the empty chair. His head is heavy and it drops slightly, changing his field of vision. He is now looking at the point where his legs go under the table. He is tired. He needs some rest. He cannot go home now, that is certain. And he cannot go back to his office—what would he do there? And how would he explain things to Dorothy? And to his junior partner Carl? No, not now. Not yet.

Year's End

He is alone in the office, Carl and Dorothy having left more than an hour ago. Just before leaving they came to wish him a happy New Year, and feeling uncomfortable, they entered his office together. He tried hard to put on his best face and even managed to grimace a sort of smile when Dorothy approached him with a kiss on the cheek. He wanted very much to be alone, and the past hour had been a relief. He is sitting at his desk, gazing at the cold rain outside, not feeling any urge to move. His mind is dull and empty and he doesn't want to think about anything in particular. Just sit and let the time pass. There is no urgency to leave for home and no New Year's Eve party to attend.

It is drizzling more softly now, as if the rain is husbanding its resources in order to last longer. Watching the puddles on the roof across the street he can almost feel the change. He imagines himself standing out there on top of that roof, face uplifted to catch the cold rain and measure its intensity. Suddenly he raises his left hand that had been lying lifeless on his thighs, and he touches his cheeks. First the right cheek, gently stroking, and then the left, unconsciously repeating the motion several times. There is something reassuring in touching himself and his hand proceeds to stroke his chin. The motion briefly focuses his attention and his gaze falls on the table in front of him.

There are several files nicely arranged on his right, and a few papers directly in front. Two of these have been there since yesterday and one since the day before yesterday. Don has started working on them several times already, but each time something crossed his mind and he lost his concentration. He is surprised at how much energy it takes to work on a single customer's file. Lately he can't muster enough of that energy. He reads with his eyes, going through the motions, even turning the pages, but not comprehending much. It feels as if his eyes are on the paper, while he himself is elsewhere.

He looks at the polished desk, observing the pale reflection of the tall black cabinet. He thinks that he can see the three thick volumes of IRS regulations reflected on his desk, but he isn't sure. Night is quickly descending and he doesn't feel like switching on the lights. He feels melancholic and in a strange way almost peaceful. It is the thought that so much has yet to be accomplished tonight before he can go to sleep that disturbs his reverie. Stand up, no, first it's necessary to make the decision to stand up, and then try to actually implement it, then stand up, collect his things, put on his coat, take the folding umbrella, shut off the lights in case they are on by then, switch on the automatic voicemail, no, that must be done with the lights still on, lock both locks, press the button for the elevator, wait for the elevator, take the elevator, and so on, and so on, an infinite number of tasks. This is too complicated, and he feels that he will never be up to it. He wonders how anyone can go on living doing all of these things on a regular basis.

Lately even eating is a major task. Although he typically orders a pizza or a hamburger to be delivered to his home, he does not feel like making the phone call, and often postpones it until he feels really hungry, or it is getting late and he worries that the restaurants will close. The voice on the other end of the line is always so business like, asking all the details about the type of pizza, and the toppings, and the size, and giving him all the family pizzas options, and he does not have the answers ready, and he feels the impatience in that voice, which makes him feel totally unwanted and inadequate. He thinks that the person on the other end of the phone must hate him by now and decides to order his food elsewhere.

These are things that Claire used to do, and she was very good at them. He wonders if restaurants are delivering takeout on New Year's Eve. He has never ordered takeout on New Year's Eve before, nor has he ordered it on Thanksgiving, or Christmas, or the Fourth of July, or, for that matter, on Yom Kippur. Not that he is truly religious, but Yom Kippur is something special just the same. Well, tonight he will find out about these things. He feels sorry for himself, and has a sudden urge to call someone. Claire? Of course not. Who knows where she is, and whether she is alone. She gave him her phone number "for emergencies," but he has not made use of it yet. The thought that a male voice may answer his call is too much for him. He often imagines himself calling her, and even tries to guess who that other person might be, and whether he knows him or not. He hopes he does not.

It is now completely dark, and he can barely see the familiar contours of his office. He has never looked at it in darkness, and it gives him an odd feeling, as if he was trespassing. He thinks that this is how his office looks every single evening after he leaves, but he never notices. Just like the thing with Claire. He was in the dark on that one too. Outside, the lights were shaking because of the rain. The puddles on the roof of the building across the street are now in pitch darkness, but he knows that there are still there. He thinks of jumping out of the window, aiming his body at those puddles. It is too far, and he would miss them by a great margin. Instead of a splash on the roof, it would be a long fall to the street below, ending with a thud. A mere thud, barely noticeable over the rush hour noise. Between the thud and the splash, he preferred the splash.

Lately such thoughts suddenly pop up in his brain without any advance notice. At first he was scared, but not anymore. At least not always. The thoughts do not seem to be his own, and they feel as if they have been planted by some external force. Most of his thoughts now appear to be like that. What sometimes scares him are not the thoughts themselves, but their tenacity, unwilling to let go. In the past he did not think much about his thoughts, and where they came from, and whether they felt like his own or not. This is a new thing and he doesn't know how to shake it off. Like the question of Claire's lover.

Don doesn't want to think about Claire's lover, but even now, as he is imagining the details of his botched suicide, his shattered body lying on the street for several long seconds before anybody noticed, he wonders what Claire's reaction would be like, and whether she would be able to go on living with her lover. He has no idea what he looks like, whether he is young or old, rich or poor, or whether he even exists. But most of the time he is sure that she must have left him for someone else. How could anybody have the courage to just leave knowing she'd be alone? No, it didn't make sense. Claire would never do a thing like that. After all, she was the pragmatic one in the family. Don knows that although he tried to take care of most of the so-called important family business—going to the bank, investing their meager savings, or planning their annual vacation—he never felt at ease doing those things. And Claire, who of course was well aware of how awkward he felt around others, tried to support him, without making it too obvious. He thought now that it was actually a shame that he never told her openly how he appreciated her efforts. Somehow it became the usual pattern between them, and he got used to it, soon taking it for granted.

Don thinks that even the act of killing himself needs to be considered from a practical point of view, otherwise it would be a mess. But there is a lot to think about before confronting that issue. For instance, there is the question of Claire's lover, and whether he prefers her to have one or not. Entire days and nights have been spent pondering this question. Even now, he is not sure which is better, to be abandoned (for that was what it was, make no bones about it) because of himself only, or because of someone else? There are times when he prefers her to live with her mythical lover, which makes her decision easier to understand. After all, she did not run away from him, but rather she ran toward someone else. The main reason for her leaving was that other person's qualities, rather than his inadequacy. But, as always, when he tries to thus comfort himself, he immediately imagines the details of her lover's qualities. The obvious advantages he has over him, Don. He knows that it will hurt, but he can't avoid imagining the couple making love. He had always thought that Claire had a healthy sexual appetite, which he found a bit too demanding. Well, her lover must be hot in bed. In fact, they are probably spending whole days in bed, with Claire making up for lost time. In the darkness of his office,

Don visualizes the details of her orgasm, listening to her deep and quick breath, her moans, her short endearments, trying to see who her lover is. This is pure torture. This is like cutting into his own flesh. He knows the feeling well, as he has often dwelled on these images before. After the sexual details comes the anger, the blind fury. He can feel it mounting in his chest, forcing him to stand up from his chair.

Pacing his office, Don thinks about his newly found energy. He knows that were it not for his anger he would never have found the strength to change his position. Perhaps now is the time to take that fatal step? But why? It's crazy, and it isn't his idea. He never invited it, and when it arrived out of nowhere, he doesn't know what to do with it. Approaching the window, he looks at the street below, but his office is so high up that the cars look like toys. The pedestrians are just tiny dots moving like so many ants this way and that. Just when some of the dots disappear, new ones take their place. Emptiness is unnatural, and is quickly filled up. That is why it is obvious that Claire has a lover. He is less angry now, and tries to think about it in a more detached manner, giving the bedroom a wide berth.

Since when has she had this liaison? How long before their parting—he knew that this was a very generous way to refer to it—had she been cheating him? Knowing Claire, she probably took her time, playing it as safely as possible under the circumstances. She wanted to check the merchandise first—he knew that the bedroom was claiming entry again, but managed to resist it just for a while longer—having learned from experience. After all, from when they first started dating until shortly after their marriage, they had been much more sexually active than later on. Don is helpless to defy the return of the images, including the expert change of positions, the multiple climaxes, and all the rest. But it is her eyes that hurt him most. He sees her beautiful dark eyes wide open, the pupils dilated with excitement, softly looking into the distance with total abandon. It has been ages since he saw that look on her face, and now, realizing that it belongs to the one who evoked it, he feels sadness sweeping him off his feet. He sat down, crossed his arms in front of him on his desk, and slowly lowered his head.

✶✶✶✶✶

Deep in his self-imposed anesthesia, the sound of the turning key reaches Don from a great distance. The first intimations of consciousness are quickly followed by the frightening awareness that someone is about to enter his office. It must be the cleaning lady. Suddenly he realizes that he is about to be caught sitting dejected in his dark office, stripped naked in his sorrow. There is no time to switch on the lights, and no time to get ready. As the door opens, he knows that he should quickly stand up to face this unexpected challenge, and try to save the last vestiges of his dignity, but he feels too tired to move. *Let me be,* he thought, *please let me be.* As the door opened he makes a halfhearted attempt to lift his head from the desk, but the onslaught of the blinding light catches him in the middle of the movement. Although almost totally blinded and blinding, he can see the terror on the face of the woman staring at the apparition in front of her.

"Oh, forgive me…I didn't know…I'm sorry…."

She is about to turn around and leave, as if it were possible to undo the entire encounter, when Don, almost shouting, says, "Don't." Just that. "Don't." But inside he hears himself saying more than that: *Please don't! Please don't leave now! Please don't leave me now!*

She hesitates, the bucket in her hand swinging from the interrupted movement. His eyes quickly adapt and the woman occupies a large segment of his visual field. It is as if he has zoomed in on her, her dark skin glowing in the brilliant light. Her thick arms are bare, her overalls are hanging loosely on her huge figure, and her chest heaves from the shock of the unexpected encounter.

"I hope I did not disturb you." And after another moment, as she has time to make a full assessment of the situation, she exclaims, "Oh, Mr. Mendelson! Is something the matter?"

Thus recognized, Don hopes that it isn't just because of the name printed on his door. He is sure that he has never seen this woman who now looks so beautiful to him. Her voice is deeply melodious and he likes the soft way in which she pronounces his name. Don feels enormous relief. Having been apprehended in his unguarded moment of grief, and caught alone in his dark office, and called by his name, he is left with nothing more to worry about. Nothing more to lose. He feels oddly free with this woman, this dark angel who came to protect him from himself. And yet, he said, "No...I'm alright, really."

Captive in the prison of social pretense, only the unnecessary "really" gives him away. That and the slowness of his speech, which sounds to him to be dragging behind him, as if a separate entity carrying a heavy load. He thought of standing up, but before he can attempt anything that major, she comes closer, and shaking her head, said, "Oh, no, Mr. Mendelson, you ain't alright. You ain't alright at all."

The distance getting smaller, he realizes that she is quite old, and wonders why a woman her age would work as a cleaning lady. *What a stupid question,* he thought, *what an utterly stupid question.* He feels for her, and when she puts down the bucket that kept making incongruous clicking sounds, and moves closer still, he said, "It is just that I am lonely." And thinking of her, he added, "Too lonely for our own good."

Coming now on his right and behind him, she clasps his head and gently presses it to her bosom. "There, that's better…that's much better." Rocking thus in her embrace, the scent of her sweat reaching him from her armpits, the unmistakable softness of her breasts cushioning his neck, Don feels the sudden swelling of emotion gathering in his lungs, and it bursts out in a crescendo of uncontrollable crying. He loses all sense of time, and abandons himself to his long-sought relief.

✳✳✳✳✳

The next morning, refreshed by what was surely the best sleep in a long while, in the comfort of his armchair facing the TV, Don skips through his now obsolete weekly calendar, and comes across a quote that he liked: "Recall it as often as you wish, a happy memory never wears out." It is by a certain Libbie Fudim. Don has never heard of Libbie Fudim, but the quote strikes a familiar chord with him. He likes to reminisce about the times he and Claire were happy, and the pleasure of those memories never seems to wear out. It is the last quote in the calendar, in the top right corner (the best, according to Don) of the week of December 27 through January 2, just above Thursday. Don has used this calendar for a year now but never noticed the quotes, perhaps because they are in the least conspicuous locations. Now that he has discovered them at the very last moment before throwing the calendar away, he starts looking at the other quotes to see if any are noteworthy. The one the week before last had Joseph Joubert saying, "Kindness consists of loving people more than they deserve." He supposes that on that account he has been kind to Claire, perhaps kind for years. Was she kind to him?

December 13 says, "If you carry your childhood with you, you never become older." He doesn't want to think about age, and skips the name under the quote. The previous week claims, "Good instincts usually tell you what to do long before your head has figured it out." His instincts tell him that Claire must have a lover, or she wouldn't have left so suddenly. After all, she never gave him a proper warning. Sure, he might have picked up a few signs here and there, but there was no verbal warning. After all these years he was entitled to an explicit warning prior to taking the ultimate destruction of their relationship.

Don feels his anger mounting. How could she not warn him at least once? It is unfair. He might have done something. He might have changed. He might have carried his childhood with him, so as to never become older. Or, as Mike Ditka rightly says on Thursday, December 2, "One is never a loser until one quits trying." At least he could have tried. But no, Claire did not want him to change. She did not want him to try and perhaps to succeed. She wanted to get him out of her life, that's what his instincts told him now, long before his head could figure it out.

Don realizes that he urgently needs professional help. Even the cleaning lady said so. "Oh, Mr. Mendelson, I thinks you should see a doctor, I really do." Was she too gentle to use the word psychiatrist, or did she avoid it out of ignorance? Of course she knew the word—it is a common word. Suddenly he realizes that he forgot to ask her name. He wanted to, but he was too shy at first, and later the opportunity to do so was somehow gone. He must ask her tonight. No, it's New Year's Day, the offices are closed, and there is no need to clean them again. And tomorrow is Saturday, so his first chance to see her will be on Monday. If she comes. If she doesn't suddenly leave without prior warning.

Don feels that he is about to enter the minefield of his thoughts again and quickly looks up for more quotations, moving backwards in time. October 14: "There are no shortcuts to any place worth going" (Beverly Sils). Next there are some stupid ones that he passes over, coming to Ingrid Bergman on August 19: "Happiness is good health and bad memory." He knows that something is wrong with this quote but can't put his finger on it. The good health part is OK, but something about bad memory isn't right. It doesn't agree with a thought that he had just a moment ago. Yes, it probably contradicts an earlier quotation that he liked. He searches the back pages but can't find it. It is only on the third attempt that he sees it on the very last page. *Must have missed it because of Libbie Fudim,* he thought, but his inability to concentrate on even the simplest tasks starts to worry him. Even Claire suggested that he should see a shrink. He is still deliberating whether to actually do it, and whether he owes it to himself and to his children, when he comes across a quote by Henry Winkler on April Fool's Day: "A human being's first responsibility is to shake hands with himself." That decided it. It is his first and only New Year's resolution, besides resolving to purchase the Oxford Book of Quotations.

March 25: "A true friend never gets in your way, unless you happen to be going down" (Arnold H. Glasgow). He wondered what the H. stands for. March 18: "The speed of the leader determines the rate of the pack" (Wayne Lukas). January 7: "Nothing makes a person more productive than the last minute" (Unknown). And finally, going back a full year, on December 31 he finds Joey Adams wishing, "May all your troubles last as long as your New Year's resolutions." For a moment Don isn't sure whether he should laugh or not.

Don likes the slight excitement that he feels shortly after reading a quote that sounds right. He measures the time and he thinks it could be felt about one second after he finished reading. The excitement is a mixture of understanding the point and evaluating its validity. It also contains an initial quick reference to himself. He is disappointed at having finished the entire year, not sure of what he should do next. Afraid of thinking about Claire's lovemaking, he searches for his new calendar, only to discover that it has no quotes. On the spur of the moment he puts on his coat and wants to go down to the drugstore to look for another calendar instead.

It is strange to be able to leave just like that without having to explain to Claire what he was about to do. He had the same feeling when he finished his breakfast and realized that there were no crumbs to collect. Claire was always a messy eater and he couldn't stand the crumbs. *Saved from these minor annoyances, I am now free to rot in my own grief*, he thought. Impressed by the honesty of this observation, Don feels that his decision to see a therapist is a timely one, and that there is no need to rush into the miserable weather outside to look for a lousy calendar. Removing his coat he switches on the TV instead.

Flipping through the channels he settles on CNN. It is the funeral procession that makes him stop there. He has always had a strong fascination with matters associated with death, including his own eventual death. The small coffin and the pastor's British accent made him think of yet another IRA bomb, but he wasn't sure. It might have been the funeral of little Jimmy brutally murdered in Liverpool by too small children. Lately he has watched a lot of TV and knows what is going on. "Time doesn't heal," said the pastor. "It only helps us to cope better."

Don is surprised by the extent to which everything and everybody is speaking directly to him. He isn't alone; he is a part—nay, an important part—of it all. And for a brief moment he feels one with the world.

A Letter from London

London, May 9

Dear Irv,

Were it not for my explicit promise to write (which, incidentally, you extracted from me against my better judgment), I wonder whether I would have had the strength to do it. I certainly don't have the appetite for writing, so it will be a short letter this time.

The red eye from New York to London was miserable. People kept walking through the aisles, the airline crew kept serving drinks, feeding us terrible food, and trying to sell us duty free items, so in spite

---

of my best efforts, I just couldn't sleep. They put us in a hotel near Oxford Street and the noise from all the traffic could easily compete with midtown Manhattan. The group went on a city tour, but I stayed behind to catch some sleep. Beyond a few short hours of a sort of twilight state, I was unsuccessful. I am mentioning these details only because you were explicit about sleep disturbances being one of the best indicators of depression. (I just had an urge to find the midpoint of this word, and couldn't go on writing before satisfying what you call one of my obsessions.) I can't judge how depressed I am, but neither my sleep nor my appetite (here again, there must be something about the sound of the words that catches me in their snares) are anything to boast about.

To be honest with you, Irv, I can't help wondering whether this entire African venture wasn't a major mistake. The others in the group seem to be too noisy for my taste. They try hard to make friends, but I just don't want to be pushed. I want to take my time and sixteen days is too short for that. In fact there are only fifteen days left, and not including the flight to Harare and then both flights back, that leaves just twelve days. So why did I insist on the shorter of the two trips? Because even this might be too much for me right now. All I really want is to be at home (alas, by myself), and to watch some stupid TV movie. To sit and not think about anything, particularly not anything about myself or about the questions that you seem to be asking me all the time. It would be just like lying on a sandy beach on one of the Caribbean (word) islands, only those are now out for me. Perhaps for good. Why does "for good" stand for forever? What is so good about it?

The leader of the group insists that we call him Mike, but I seem unable to socialize that easy. He is too good looking and too young for my taste, and probably quite inexperienced. I keep recalling the stories of white hunters absolutely having to sleep with the client's wives, almost as if it was a part of the deal. This Mike certainly did not waste any time in surveying the landscape, and he tries hard to impress the ladies, particularly a young blonde named Iris. She seems to be alone and I wonder what made a woman like her join this particular trip.

I might well be among the oldest in our group, but it is too early to tell. I certainly feel I'm being old and useless and altogether down. Claire (I wish I could say "damn her," but there is no anger in my heart, only sadness) would have enjoyed this thing much more than I can ever expect to, but I was too stupid to grant her her wish. She would surely be quite cynical when she learns that I have finally been to London. Would she think that by leaving me she caused me to also feel suddenly liberated? That is so far from the truth that nothing could be more unfair. But it would make her feel better, so she probably would believe it.

Claire, all the time Claire. Wherever I look I see her. Whenever I listen I hear her. This morning, at the airport, a certain Mr. So-and-So was called to the information desk. The voice of the announcer was just like Claire's, and for a moment I had an urge to actually go to the information desk. As I was waiting for my suitcase, I waited to hear yet another announcement by her, but in vain. Then, just as I was leaving the customs area, I thought she came on again, but the voice was too faint to be sure.

You told me that I should not be afraid of missing Claire, and that it would do me more good than trying to quickly push her out of my mind. Well, on that account, I can assure you that I have more than I need, and perhaps much more than is good for me. After all, it has been several months now since she left, and I miss her more than ever before. And do you know what? I hope I will never stop missing her. I will miss missing her. You see, Doctor, by hurting me, she is still a part of me.

[Wanting to sign off, Don didn't know how to end this first letter to his therapist. There were simply too many possibilities. "Your friend" was too pretentious. "Always" had no place in this early stage of their correspondence. "Sincerely" was cold and formal. It was only after a long struggle that he could resolve his problem, signing:]

Best,

Don

Dusk

He positioned himself well. The sun still had about an hour to go, but by now he knew the exact spot, at the top of the second tree from the edge, where it will settle. Yesterday he miscalculated slightly and was quite surprised when the huge red ball barely touched the treetops, and quickly disappeared in the open space between the two trees. He did not want that. *Sunsets should make use of trees,* he thought, *particularly bare trees, with their branches providing the proper backdrop for the evening drama.*

And drama it undoubtedly was. That time of day when the African light first becomes strikingly golden, then a gentler yellow gradually fading and turning to brown, that is also the time for all the animals to fear what lies ahead. For the night in Africa is one of predation. *Like in the city jungles,* he thought, *but more sudden, swifter, and much cleaner.*

He also fears the night, but mostly because of the stars and the solitude they imply. But there is still plenty of time before darkness, and today he is prepared. From the position of his chair he can observe not only the sun that is just beginning to change color, but also the entire Sinamatella plain below. He can see the Sinamatella River meandering in gentle curves, and the few spots that still have water are well within sight. Farther south, the thicker vegetation of the Lukasi River is marked by deeper silver, and lifting his gaze toward the far distance he can see the tops of the remote hills all the way to the Kalahari. He likes the sound of the word Kalahari; it suggests excitement and adventure. He likes the sound of Sinamatella as well, though in a different way. It is much more feminine, and more personal. *Sin-ama—Stop it!* Yes, after this last week, Sinamatella is clearly becoming a part of him. It is as if by making the decision to stay here for a while longer, he is gradually taking possession.

There is a large herd of buffalo directly below him on the plain, and their huge black bodies stand out even to the naked eye. When they first made their entry from the left, at about 10:30 a.m., he spent a great deal of time watching them through his binoculars. It was a good herd, two hundred and sixteen by his count, and he particularly liked to observe the huge bulls that stood guard in front and on the periphery. Huge bulls could be seen at the end of the herd as well— *tailing Charlie,* he thought—and thus the females and the calves were protected from all sides. After having watched them for several hours, he lets his eyes rest, and is surprised to note that by looking at the herd as a whole, rather than at some individuals, he can see things that had escaped him before.

Thus, for instance, there is the question of movement. Since there is clearly no single leader at the front—"The speed of the leader determines the rate of the pack," or something like that, according to one of the quotes from his old calendar—he wonders what makes the herd move in a particular direction. From the vantage point of his natural balcony, it looks like a complex coordination of many individuals. *As if the entire herd had a mind of its own,* he thought. Now, about forty minutes before sunset, the herd is clearly heading west, and if it maintains its present course and speed, its front will soon disappear behind the bend.

There are numerous elephants roaming the plain. Some are feeding, while others are drinking. To his left, not far from the clear stretch of water, four elephants are standing, heads together, neither drinking nor feeding. It looked like socializing, or like a consultation of some sort. Three of them have been standing like this for some time before the fourth, a particularly large bull, joined them. The latecomer is all glistening from wallowing in the muddy water. Some of the buffaloes are glistening as well, particularly those that were directly in the path of the sun. The wet elephant turns and starts to walk back the way he came. It is like watching something in slow motion. By now he knows something of the grace of these creatures, but there are many things he doesn't know yet and is glad to discover.

I wish I knew what all this was about, he thought, trying to imagine the kinds of things that the elephants might communicate to each other.

He thinks of Claire, and wishes that someone was here to talk to. *Even one of the tourists would do,* he thought. *With certain things it almost doesn't matter whom one is talking to. Expressing one's wonder about the elephants is one such thing…well, I can always talk to myself.* He muses about this for a while, not sure that it is the same thing.

Claire used to be a good companion. They would go places together, make all the insignificant comments to each other, and thoroughly enjoy themselves. It took several years before she started to lose patience with him. These were good years, as good as anyone can expect. And even later, when she became less tolerant of his "crazy thoughts," it was not as if he suddenly became impossible, and they still had good times together.

He doesn't want to think about Claire; at least, not just yet. He needs time to heal, and he feels that this place might be able to nurse him back to health.

Places don't heal, he chastised himself, *they don't do anything for you. Nothing and nobody can do anything worthy for you, only you can... people and places can make it more difficult or less difficult for you, that's all. This place might make it less difficult for me to do what has to be done.*

The head of the buffalo herd had begun to move beyond his line of sight behind the bend to the right, not far from where the sun would settle. He is aware of this even while thinking his thoughts about Claire and himself, and when the first two black patches disappear, he stands up for a while, trying to see them just once more. *That's cheating,* he thought, and sat back, letting go. It is hard to let go. Now that about six or seven more buffaloes are lost to him, and more are disappearing by the second, the urge to restore the picture back to its original gets stronger. He knows that in the past—oh, the so recent past—he wouldn't have been able to resist the compulsion to bring the herd to order. But this late afternoon, the seventh after his great decision, he struggles well, and with the help of the sun that suddenly seems to come down faster and deepen its color, he comes out victorious, and stays put.

✳✳✳✳✳

This great decision, what was it all about? And how could Don Mendelson, of all people, suddenly make such a far-reaching and totally unexpected move? To his friends, Don epitomizes the settled and the orderly and predictable course of life. His career as a CPA suits him well. There are few professions calling for the degree of conservatism of a CPA. Year in and year out he would work on the books of the firms that were his clients, making sure they were in good order and would stand up to the strictest scrutiny.

It is only during April that his work becomes more exciting. First there is the crazy rush to beat the IRS deadline of April 15, working around the clock with little or no sleep, followed by the traditional two weeks' vacation "to recuperate." Irrespective of how strongly he urges his clients to provide him with the necessary information well in advance, the last-minute craze just can't be avoided. And thus, on April 16, entirely spent and high on too much caffeine, Don would take Claire to the Caribbean "to recuperate, and catch some sun after the long winter."

When the children were small they used to take them along, but later, when school vacations did not coincide with the IRS deadline, they would leave them with Claire's parents and go by themselves. Don liked to be thrifty with their money, and always chose their island very carefully. Typically he would spend a few weekends in January and February studying the travel section of the *New York Times*, comparing prices, making notes of restaurants and numerous practical details, and by the end of February, when quite a few New Yorkers were taking their Caribbean vacation to really escape the winter, Don had it all planned and reserved, waiting for April 16.

For several years in a row Claire tried to suggest that they go in mid-winter, rather than in the spring, but Don would have nothing of it. "Besides," he argued, "they charge outrageous prices during the peak season." Later, Claire grew tired of going to what appeared to her essentially the same place again and again, and asked whether they couldn't go someplace else, like Europe, perhaps Paris or Florence, just once in a while. However, the idea of taking a long overnight flight and then going from one museum to another sounded to Don like absolute madness, especially after all his hard work. Besides, if you like something, why look for something else? He liked his off-season Caribbean vacations and could see no reason for changing a good, well-established tradition.

His friends used to joke about this, suggesting that he behaved like an old man, that there was no excitement in his life, that he left no room for spontaneity, change, or surprise, and more such nonsense. "What do you want me to do," he would ask, a mischievous smile hovering above his upper lip, "have a love affair?"

He loved Claire and did not need an affair. He liked his work and did not need a change. He liked his routine and found comfort in it. All around him he saw families torn apart, lives taking a sudden dangerous spin, getting out of control. This type of excitement was not for him. Not for him and Claire. And now it turned out that all this time, throughout all those years, he had no idea what was going on in her head. That more than anything else hurt him now. It was as if he had been married to a stranger. As if all his love and feelings of intimacy had suddenly turned out to be totally false. *Or simply unrequited,* he thought during his braver moments.

And yet, sitting above the vast plain, the last patches of orange in the west giving way fast, it is not the thought of being unloved that frightens him. Maybe because he knows that there was love there before. What truly terrifies him is the idea of pretense, of not knowing what was going on. After all, the transition from love to indifference took place in front of his eyes, in his very bedroom. *Maybe because it happened gradually,* he thought, *spreading over several years, I couldn't see it until a week ago.* Don often thinks about this decision and wonders who made it. Was it his, did it somehow materialize from some inner source having been long in the making? Anyhow, these inner sources, whatever they may be, were they not his? It is a problem only if you insist on understanding a decision by searching for one particular cause. *But, as Irving would say, anything we do has many causes. Like the movement of the herd of buffaloes,* he thought.

He wishes Irving could see him now. It was Irving, after all, who had sent him to Africa in the first place. What a strange thing for a therapist to do. But then Irv isn't, of course, an ordinary shrink. *He talks too much—aren't they supposed to just sit there and let you do all the work?—he gets excited, everything reminds him of a story, and he altogether seems to be enjoying himself throughout their sessions.* Don often wonders about Irv, and wishes that it was only with him that he acted this freely, while at the same time knowing only too well that it has absolutely nothing to do with him. *Unless it was my dullness that provoked him,* he thought, but even that was probably too presumptuous.

"What would you like to do when you grow up?" This favorite question of his used to bother Don more than he cared to admit. "What do you mean you don't know? Don't you have dreams, secret wishes, and fantasies?" The truth, however, was that Don has considered himself a grown-up for many years now, but when he said so, Irv, at that time still Dr. Irving Hunt, started shouting at him: "Must I spell it all out for you? OK then, I will. So tell me, Don, what would you like to do before dying? Is there anything at all that you would still like to do before it's too late?"

Having failed coming at him from the start, he was now trying to get at him from the end. What a dirty trick. Why, grown up, yes, but old and dying—that was too much for Don. He considered himself a reasonably healthy middle-aged man, with an occasional backache and case of the flu, a little overweight, nothing special. And certainly there was nothing signifying any imminent danger. *Unless it creeps up on you unnoticed, just like Claire did. Yes, cancer can do that to you, spreading over the course of several years, and the rest of it, just like Claire did.*

He doesn't like these thoughts and wishes they would stop bothering him so often. Lifting his gaze he can see the beginning of what promised to be yet another wonderful starry night. There is no pollution in Sinamatella and there are no city lights to compete with the skies. Besides, Irv was right when he said that once you cross the equator into the southern hemisphere, it is a totally different ball game. Thousands of bright starts that can't ever be seen in the north suddenly appear side by side with some familiar ones. *Irv was certainly right on this one,* he thought, *although he did not mention the Milky Way.* Don could see the Milky Way most nights. But even while pondering the beauty above him, he knows that sooner or later he will have to come back down to seriously consider the thoughts that made him escape upwards. This awareness is a new thing to him. Screening the heavens above, he can feel it in the tension of his neck.

He is looking for the Southern Cross but can't find it. Why, yesterday it was right on the imaginary line between the exact spot where the sun went down and himself. He likes to think of himself as searching for the Southern Cross, in a way that many a sailor must have done over the centuries. But no matter how much he tries, he can't find it. For a brief moment he thought that he had it, but then it vanished. *Maybe I changed the position of my chair too much from yesterday,* he thought, and tries to move it this way and that, but without success. *Could it be that the stars move that much in a single day? It doesn't make sense at all, and besides, if it were moving that much, the Southern Cross would have had no navigational value at all. Nothing is stable anymore, nothing.*

Suddenly he feels cold, and realizes that it is now almost pitch dark. There is light coming from the window of the few occupied cabins and more light from the restaurant, but there is absolutely nothing on the vast plain below, throughout Hwange National Park all the way to Kalahari. *That has not changed for thousands of years, or more,* he thought. The real Africa, his Africa, he would like to think, is stable. It is the only thing stable enough to lean on without worrying whether it will shift without prior warning. He is very lucky to have discovered this place. Now that he has found it, he should make use of it, before, as Irv would say, it is too late.

Lions

Sinamatella, May 23

Dear Irv,

I keep wondering about sequences. Somehow it seems to me that if the African trip did not start at Victoria Falls, moving through Robins Camp to Sinamatella, but the other way around, I would now be on my way back home. Perhaps even already in the office. For some reason my office is presenting itself as the direct antithesis to this place. You see, if I had started here, it probably wouldn't have meant a thing, just a beautiful lookout on the plain below. I needed the Falls to attract my attention, to pull me out of my cocoon of self-pity, and by their sheer force to penetrate under my skin. They acted as a bombardment in battle, softening up the enemy position. Then came Robins Camp, the morning walks and the evening fires, and the starry nights, and, of course, the lions. I must have mentioned them before, but let me describe the event in some detail.

There were twelve of us, including the local guide, who fortunately carried a gun. After explaining the basics of walking in the bush, he looked us over and picked me to be "tailing Charlie," adding with a smile that the last position in the line is sometimes called "hyena bait" as well. I could not stop wondering why he chose me of all the men in our group, since the rest were much younger and certainly looked fitter. I was flattered and in my vanity threw a quick glance at Iris to see how she took this. You used to complain that I am too defensive about sex, so I hope this last remark will show you that I have made some progress. You see, Iris is one of those blondes that no man can truly disregard. Although throughout the trip I exchanged with her only the perfunctory good mornings (no good evenings, mind you), several nice day todays, and an occasional how are you, with hardly any question mark at its end, I liked to watch her from a safe distance. I doubt that she even noticed, since women like her must be used to men staring at them all the time.

As soon as we started walking, it was clear that there were too many of us. We made too much noise and whenever the guide stopped in order to explain something about the tracks or the terrain, by the time the "tail" approached the head, he had usually finished. He spoke in very short sentences and never even looked at his audience. It was as if he was enjoying the walk and his expertise of the bush, but could just as well talk to himself. Suddenly I envied this guide. With little formal schooling, if any, he seemed totally in his element, and fully absorbed by what he saw, heard, and smelled. Yes, Irv, I envied his being so unconscious of himself, so in touch with his world. And I imagined the way he must look forward to each morning, in spite of the stupid questions that tourists like us asked him occasionally.

I tried to put myself in his shoes (high boots, worn out by years of walking in the bush, laces only loosely tied together) and again looked at Iris who was walking second in line, right behind him. We were walking downhill now, and if he had stopped suddenly, she would have practically bumped into him. Imagine, Irv, on this clear morning I found myself actually trying to feel the collision that might be thus produced. And what if he would stop and quickly turn around at the same time? He was lucky. Can you believe that it is me writing this? However, I feel that it is important not only as an indication of what you would call the first intimations of the rebirth of my long dormant and now bleeding libido, but especially in view of what followed.

In retrospect, I think that I was simply drunk by my senses. You see, it all started with getting up just as the sun was about to rise, smelling the fresh cool air, drinking the scalding strong coffee while standing close to the remnants of last night's fire, feeling the warmth slowly spreading across my entire body. The many birds resting in the trees around the camp started their morning calls, and even the wild dove could be heard. The group was slowly drifting from the bungalows toward the fire, softly greeting each other. Not everybody was up for the morning walk, which gave those of us who were a feeling of being both virtuous and adventurous.

I was particularly glad to see that Mike was not coming, although my feeling had no objective basis whatsoever. It was just one of those automatic things that gets hold of you for no apparent reason and does not listen to reason. (Why is one reason related to the other? It must have happened long before psychoanalysis.) Actually, he was a very kind person and turned out to be much more knowledgeable about life in the bush than I expected. Well tanned, always wearing his fashionable khaki shorts, a green scarf around his neck, he quickly became the darling of our group. It must have been his casual manner, being at ease with the others that I disliked. That and the scarf. With Mike around there was no room left for a hopeless introvert like myself. Needless to say, the guide would surely have chosen him to be "tailing Charlie." In his absence I could breathe more freely.

Breathing, Irv, is the right word for it. On this clear and crisp morning, with the light first turning golden and then extravagantly bright, the sheer physical pleasure of inhaling the African air was intoxicating. It was while thus intoxicated that I guarded the rear of our column against hyenas, and on occasion indulged in watching the newly discovered beauty of a woman from a safe distance.

The guide took us to a wet and muddy area, where he found some perfect pug marks of a lion. He said that they were quite fresh and decided to follow the tracks. The realization that we were now stalking a lion sent waves of excitement throughout our group and we were now more silent and alert to our immediate surroundings. The lucky guide walked quite fast for someone who had to look for signs of direction and I was impressed. Once in a while he would stop and show us the marks on the ground, or the broken stalks of grass indicating the lion's passage. He whispered and from my rear position I couldn't hear anything. Passing by the place where he made the remarks I would desperately search the ground for something, anything, but usually without success. I wished I was closer to him (and her) to hear what he had to say.

We had now been walking for some time and the sun was getting hot. I started to sweat on my brow and under my arms, and from time to time I would wipe my forehead and smell my hand. I liked the smell of my sweat. It was something intimate between me and my body; something that I experienced only rarely. Iris wore a beige shirt with two pockets in front, one on each side. I wondered whether she kept something in those pockets and how it felt putting it there. She probably had to exhale and stop breathing throughout the entire action. I tried to catch sight of her armpits to check for sweat, but she didn't wave her hands enough, and even if she did, she was probably too far anyway. Perhaps if I stood close to her I would be able to smell her sweat. I read somewhere that everyone has a slightly different smell, and that is what causes attraction or repulsion without our being aware of the reason. Just like dogs sniffing each other.

Suddenly Lucky stopped in his tracks, crouched close to the ground, and motioned us to do the same. Although it was sudden, Iris managed to avoid the much contemplated collision. That happened further along the line, producing a chain effect similar to the Long Island Expressway on a misty night. Or the effect of adding a suffix to a word whose center you had previously determined. At first there is no problem, but suddenly the letters start bumping into each other, causing a major disturbance around the middle. You were right about the richness of our associations. We carry our worlds in our heads, where they wait for a chance to express themselves.

But I mustn't keep you in suspense since the drama was already upon us. The commotion within our line had barely settled down when not far from us, in a small clearing in the bush, we saw a lioness. The bright light made her look larger than life, and from her nervous pacing she was obviously irritated with our clumsy approach. Then she gave a minor grunt, and without any warning—just like Claire— she attacked. Make no mistake; it was a full-blown charge across the space between us, accelerating in the process. Within two seconds she was halfway through, when Lucky fired a shot above her head. We were just as shocked by the sound of the gun as she must have been, because it broke her charge and after she slid with the momentum of her movement—it was now her turn to imitate the LIE traffic—the shot stopped her right in her tracks. She was very close now and after several irritated grunts turned around and disappeared into the dense bush.

The whole episode took a few seconds and there was no time to get scared. It was only after the danger had passed that I felt my heart racing like mad in my chest. It was a near miss alright, and I couldn't understand why it had happened. Lions are not supposed to attack people just like that without clear provocation. Our group was now talking loudly, in order to relieve the tension. Someone shouted that he had filmed the charge. "I had her right in focus and the camcorder picked up the sound of the shot as well." Even Lucky was obviously shaken, and after surveying the bush with his binoculars he quickly turned around and led us away. It was odd playing the mad lioness bait at the end of the column.

After putting some distance between her and us, Lucky found some open space, stopped, and looked at us for the first time. We pushed close to him, waiting for his opinion. There was a strong odor of sweat hanging about our closely packed group, most of it due to fear. I found myself not far from where Iris stood, a few paces behind her, observing the two pockets covering the rear of her slacks, noting the she probably couldn't use those under any circumstances.

"This lioness is too cheeky," said our guide, "we must have disturbed her mating."

"But we didn't see a male lion," somebody ventured.

"The male is probably too tired to bother with us," said Lucky with a mischievous smile.

"Can't we go back and look? Please!" This was from Iris. She said it so quickly, and her plea was so coquettish, that I knew immediately that Lucky had no choice in the matter. Other voices now joined in, pleading with our guide to take us back so we could have the opportunity to see and film the lions' lovemaking.

"I don't know, this lioness is too cheeky." But he didn't struggle for long, and after reloading his gun, he led us back. This time, however, he chose a more prudent approach. Sifting some sand between his fingers he determined the direction of the wind and started to make a long circle that would bring us to them from upwind. I felt oddly tense, and not entirely convinced by his explanation. Maybe there is no male, just a mad female charging anything in sight. At the same time I was scared of watching this female's lovemaking, fearing that it would bring back some of the images that were haunting me for so many months. It was a foolish thought, but I couldn't help myself.

The circle we made was a long one, and by the time we got near to the place of the attack it was well past the time we were scheduled to return to camp. The sun was already high and it was quite hot. Lucky avoided the dense bush where the cheeky lioness would have had a clear advantage, and chose a route without any shade. I was thirsty but didn't dare stop for a drink. There would be time for that later. On our right were several female waterbucks, wary of our approach. They did not run away, but moved just fast enough to maintain a comfortable distance. Lucky stopped us and explained that he didn't want the waterbucks to alert the lions to our presence. We waited, but they stopped as well, unwilling to let us go out of their sight. For several minutes it was a stalemate, when suddenly they snorted and jumped into the dense bush. "Must have smelled the lions," explained our guide, who was sweating profusely. I thought of drinking now, but decided against it, and felt very virtuous, almost as if I had just successfully resisted the urge to find the midpoint of a particularly long word. We all waited for the drama to unfold.

Suddenly we heard the unmistakable roar of a male lion. It was very loud, and during the peak of its bass note the earth appeared to shake. I could not help myself from visualizing the opening of a Metro Goldwyn Meyer movie, although the real roar was longer, ending with several short grunts, which were entirely missing in the MGM version. They sounded like aftershocks. It was as if the lion could not make the transition from total domination of the surrounding area to one of silence without some intermediate steps.

Slowly, crouching low, we advanced into the thicket. Was this reckless? Had our guide unwisely yielded to pressure from a few foolish tourists? I wished Claire could have seen her timid CPA now, guarding the rear of our column. Exposed to danger. Bending low without giving my lower back a thought. For it is only now, while writing this account in the comfort of this armchair, with the extra support of a well-placed cushion, that the image of what might have happened were I to get one of those lumbar spasms right there, occurred to me for the first time.

Here, my esteemed confessor, I had to stop writing, because I got entirely caught up with the details of that scene— "tailing Charlie" unable to follow the group, unwilling to shout for them to stop, finding himself alone in a semi-crouching position unable to move, wild animals everywhere, but most of all, and unbearable *hum-ill-iat-ion*, the *mor-tif-i-cat-ion*, the *emb-arr-a-ssm-ent*!!!

Then I saw them. At first I could only see the male with his huge black mane, reclining on the boulder at the opposite end of the clearing. The lioness was nowhere to be seen. So naturally did she blend in with the golden colors of the dry grass that it was only when she moved that I could see her too. And what a movement that was. Irv, you should have seen that lioness move. Her back was undulating like several sinusoid curves merging into each other. In slow motion, slightly low, but not so low as to touch the ground like when stalking prey—it was a different kind of prey she was after now—in a few gliding steps she approached her partner, and gently rubbed her side and her cheek against his. The thought that "this lioness was too cheeky" was forming itself in my mind, but didn't yet fully cross my consciousness, which was totally enthralled by the sight.

With the last part of her body released from its long rubbing motion, she turned around and rubbing now with her other side terminated the movement by presenting her rear in front of him. And what was he doing all this time? The moment he saw her approach he lifted his head, and when she rubbed against him he stood up and proceeded to mount her from behind, his back making a perfect arc against the blue sky. The act itself was short, and after a few thrusts he bit her neck, and signaled his climax by repeating the majestic roar we had heard before. She returned to the tall grass where she lay down playfully on her back, pawing the air like a kitten. He reclined on the huge boulder, just like when we had first seen him.

The intensity of the roar accentuated the silence that followed. The only sound was the swishing of the dry grass by the lioness. We broke our single file and slowly pressed closer to each other. Several cameras were still jostling for position when the lioness started her undulating movement once more. As if hypnotized we watched her make the same approach, rubbing first one way and then another, and her mate unable to resist the invitation gathering his strength, lifting himself up, mounting her, and thrusting his pelvis into that sleek body. I stood not far from Iris and could hear her catching her breath, her shirt about to burst, and then when the lion bit the nape of his partner's neck, I saw her bite her lower lip. When the by now inevitable roar came, she looked at me, and realizing that I had seen everything, released a sigh of her own.

We now shared a bond formed by our common secret, and nothing could be the same again. We observed the act repeat itself numerous times within an hour, all the while watching each other as well. The sheer energy spent by the magnificent male was matched by the temptation that made it possible. It was obvious that he was her prisoner, unable to resist her advances. I felt young and vigorous, and oddly elated by everything that had taken place. It was as if on this hot morning my journey to Sinamatella had begun.

Best,

Don

Mirror

Don never sends a letter before reading it again at least once. He likes to think that it is his CPA training that makes him do that, but by now he knew better. He is sitting in the straw armchair in his cabin, close to the shaded lamp that cast its weak yellow light on the block of paper on his lap. Having just finished reading his long letter to Irv, he is well aware that the ending is incorrect. His journey to Sinamatella had not started the morning he saw the lion. It had started several months ago, in the office of Dr. Irving Hunt, psychotherapist extraordinaire.

While the decision to seek help was his own, the therapist was one suggested by Claire, during one of her rare phone calls "to update him" about the children. She had been seeing him for more than two years now and was very satisfied. Don couldn't believe his ears. Two years? And he didn't know a thing about it? Another case of something done in secrecy. And the money? Where did she get the money for it? Must have cost fortune. Assuming three sessions per week makes twelve a month at a minimum of, say, $70 per session, or, if this Hunt person is so good even an even hundred per session, it came to $1,200 a month, and a total of $28,800 over the course of two years. If she saw him four times a week, and knowing Claire was prone to take everything that she set her mind to very seriously, four times a week it was, that makes a total of $38,400. A fortune. His money earned by hard labor and put into their joint account in complete trust. How come he never noticed anything missing? A wonderful CPA he was. Oddly, he hadn't mentioned money during that phone conversation; it surfaced in all its strength later. He thought about Claire's power over him; just hearing her voice was enough to distract him to the point of helplessness.

And what about the changes in Claire herself? If the therapy was so good for her she must have changed somehow during its course, but being totally blind he hadn't noticed. Suddenly Don is struck by the possibility, nay, the certainty that her therapy must have played a role in her decision to leave him. Perhaps it had been this shrink himself who suggested it in the first place. *Your husband is not good for you and you are still too young to ruin the rest of your life,* Don could hear him saying. In his mind, her vehement protests were soon reduced to mere *I'll have to think about it,* later the worry that *Don would be utterly devastated, I can't do this to him,* and then the realization that *it's my life anyway, and I probably should've done this a long time ago.*

What Don likes about this particular scenario is the total absence of a lover. It is between her and the shrink that the plot takes shape and there is no need to think about his sexual prowess. It is just a case of marital incompatibility. It took only twenty-four years to realize it, but now that it is in the open, there is no question about it. *I am glad you made me understand this,* she must have told him in a moment of revelation.

So now Don is curious about this person, and since Claire had always been the more practical one, he decides to give it a try. *Besides,* he thought, *since Claire must have talked a great deal about me, it will save a lot of time and money. But what if she told him the wrong things? What if the way she perceives me is totally wrong?* Well, in that case he would at least have a chance to put things right. *A sort of poetic justice,* thought Don, and he called to make an appointment.

✷✷✷✷✷

Elephants. Loads of them. A huge herd occupies the centerpiece of the main wall across from the bookshelf. The herd attracts his attention more than the standard rows of books. It consists of about fifteen of the huge beasts walking on a dusty plain. The light is very soft and Don thinks the picture must have been taken at sunset. The sunset is not in the picture, but its presence is felt all over. To the left of this panoramic scene is a close-up of a single elephant reaching toward a tall branch of a dead tree. Above him, in black and white, are a mother and her baby. The baby has no tusks and looks funny. Don suspects that there must be more elephants behind him, but he does not feel comfortable enough to turn his head.

"Do you like my elephants?"

"Yes," says Don, knowing that the answer came out too automatically to sound sincere. He hadn't yet had time to look at them closely, and isn't sure that he likes them. "Did you take those pictures?"

"Yes."

"In Africa?"

"Yes. These are African elephants. Indian elephants are smaller, and their spines look different."

"When did you visit Africa?"

There is a deep sigh and a pause before he answers, "Oh, the last time was long ago. Too long ago. Almost a full year now."

Don doesn't like the nostalgic air of his to-be therapist and doesn't pursue this line of conversation any further. Instead, he tries to take a good look at him.

Bushy eyebrows over dark eyes. The eyebrows all over the face, very thick and mostly unruly. Don doesn't know whether to look at the eyes or at the mass of darkness above them. A good forehead, on the high side, particularly due to the receding hairline, but not too high yet. The black hair very curly, in line with the eyebrows. Do all the hairy places on a man's body look the same? Don has to thrust aside some images that push themselves into his consciousness, knowing too well that once they get a proper foothold it will be an almost impossible task. He should talk about this problem of his to the person sitting comfortably in the armchair below the elephants. He should explain that in his own case there can be no doubt that rather than a foothold the unwanted images are nothing less than a bridgehead. They consist of the first serious intimation of a full-blown invasion by alien thoughts.

Help comes when Hunt turns his head and presents Don with his profile. The nose is quite long but very straight, almost perfectly so. The initial hope that in spite of having such an inappropriate name Hunt might be Jewish is now shattered by that nose. By the elephants too. Don considers himself totally open-minded about ethnicity, but the idea of unburdening himself in front of not only a total stranger, but also a gentile, seems odd. He forgot to ask Claire about this. The hair still provides some hope. Unless he styles it into an afro because of this Africa fetish. This might explain his name as well, provided it is assumed. *Must be totally nuts,* thought Don, and suddenly he feels relaxed for the first time since his arrival.

"So, Dr. Hunt, shall we give it a try?"

"Certainly…but there is no need to rush."

Don could have sworn that his question caught him entirely by surprise. Otherwise why this nonsense about there being no need to rush? Of course he won't mind carrying this on forever, given his hourly rate, but Don can think of better ways to throw away his money. For instance, he could…

He tries hard, but nothing particular comes to mind. It is as if suddenly he can't think of anything else to do with his money. To his great surprise, he feels as if there is nothing at all that he wishes to do. Money or no money, there is simply nothing that he wants to do, and nowhere that he wants to be. It is a frightening experience, as if he is dead already.

"No, Dr. Hunt, there is a need to rush. A great need indeed. I feel dead, and unless you help me quickly I will surely kill myself. The other evening I almost jumped out the window. I had this strong urge to finish everything, and if not for some last minute chance intervention, I might have done it."

Don doesn't know where all this is coming from. He had no intention of revealing his suicidal thoughts, which he himself considers mild and unconvincing. It was as if these statements were suddenly pulled out of him in spite of himself. Don could have killed himself right there and then for making such a fool of himself. *Like an awkward elephant charge,* he thought. It was so uncharacteristic of him. He hates drama, and he hates overstatement, and before coming to this place he was sure that it would take several months before he felt confident enough to say anything really personal. Now, totally bewildered by what has happened, he tries to pull himself together and keep quiet.

But it isn't purely a matter of embarrassment, for at the same time Don feels an enormous relief, as if a heavy weight has lifted from his chest. With the exception of the cleaning lady, and Don isn't sure to what extent that is indeed an exception since he isn't sure what it was in the first place, now is the first time that he has mentioned any of this to anybody. It is as if having said it, the thing is not his responsibility anymore. At least not only his.

However, that isn't all, and he is slowly becoming aware of yet another odd feeling, one of being vindicated. For he was now acquitted of all the charges Claire must have made against him in this room. His shyness, his inability to express emotion, the distance he keeps from everything and everyone, and above all, his terribly boring *predictability,* all proven wrong. In a single sweep he has shown this person that his preconceptions about the husband of his beautiful client are all inaccurate.

Hunt looks composed, moves his chair a few inches closer—*body language,* thought Don, suddenly feeling very competent in matters of the mind—and gives his new client a very long look.

"This is good," he says, slightly overdoing the length of the *gooood.* And after a brief pause, "Veeeery good."

Don doesn't like the ease with which the therapist regained control over the situation by giving marks to his client, even if they are good marks. It signifies to him a quality that he can never possess. Always self-conscious, social grace is something that he can only admire from a distance. Whenever someone tells the old joke about the difference between a *shlemiel* and a *shlemazel* he wonders which one of them describes him better. This is usually followed by telling himself that he is none of the above. Rather, he thinks of himself primarily as an awkward person. Don wonders whether psychologists view awkwardness as a diagnostic category. He could never understand how any thinking person could not be awkward. Well, Claire wasn't too awkward, certainly not by his standards.

"I am sorry about my outburst, Doctor—I feel very awkward now."

Don has no idea where the "Doctor" came from, but he realizes that by clearly putting him in the dominant position his own actions are somehow more excusable. Well, perhaps he isn't a total loss in social circumstances, although this is much too complex. He knows of complexity well enough; it is simplicity that he envies.

"You probably couldn't help it," is the reply, but it catches him in the middle of calculating the midpoint of *awk-w-ard*. He can't help himself from evoking his stupid habit, and wonders whether the time will ever come when he tells his therapist about it. He is struck by the fact that it is easier to talk about his suicidal thoughts than about his methodical dissection of words.

"There are too many things I cannot help myself from doing. Just too many." It is Don's turn now to speak slowly as befits the philosophical mode. He sees himself as the other must see him: badly dressed, slightly balding, spectacles taking up much of his face, clean shaven but without aftershave lotion, large nose, thick lips, pale complexion, sitting awkwardly, making use of barely half of what the comfortable chair had to offer.

"So what stopped you?"

"What do you mean?"

"What stopped you from killing yourself?"

Don is not ready to be pushed like this. Therapy is not supposed to be carried out by brute force. But in the silence of the room, surrounded by elephants, he tries to concentrate on answering the question. He isn't sure what stopped him, since he isn't even sure that he was at any time seriously considering doing it. It was more like a sort of game that he played with himself. Or, rather, a game that was played on him.

"I'm not sure. I guess I thought about my children." Don knows this is a lie, since he can't remember when he last thought of them. It is as if they had vanished. And yet, he loves them, and wouldn't want to hurt them, or embarrass them. Now that he thinks about it, it makes good sense.

"You did?" The Grand Inquisitor seemed unconvinced.

"I must have."

"Do you actually remember having thought about them then?"

"I think so, but I can't be absolutely sure. I was too anxious, and you can't expect me to recall everything that went through my head."

"But this is very important, since whatever it was that prevented you from killing yourself is the essence of what gives meaning to your life."

Don can understand his logic but is too preoccupied with the sound of *ipso facto*, since whatever it is that prevented him from jumping toward that wet concrete was ipso facto the essence of what gave his life meaning. He can never resist an opportunity like that, and he wonders whether the Grand Inquisitor is aware of the beauty of some Latin expressions. He should tell him about it sometime later. After all, they are supposed to spend long hours together talking about anything that comes up. The urge to go back to the two words and search for their combined midpoint was building up, but there was not enough time for that.

"I do remember worrying about making a mess of it. And about missing the spot. I mean…not doing it right."

"Is doing things right very important to you?"

"Very important. Too important. It is a constant need that I must obey." He thinks of using *prerogative*, but somewhere along the way it changed to *need*. Don is acutely aware of how much time there is to think between words. Speech is so much slower than thought that it is difficult to keep ideas in focus.

"Please entwine the fingers of both hands together. Like this." The hippie with the bushy eyebrows demonstrates how to do it. Don, taken aback by this sudden turn, follows the instructions.

"Good. Now do it the other way."

"What do you mean the other way?"

"Instead of the right thumb on top, try the left."

Don fumbled with his hands, until he managed to do it.

"How does it feel?"

"It's odd, it doesn't feel right."

"Does it bother you?"

"Yes. It does bother me slightly. I don't think that I have ever done it this way before."

At first it felt as if they were not his hands. He presses them at various points of contact, and after a while they become his. He unlaces them and brings them together again the natural way. It is such a pleasant feeling, like homecoming. He tries the other way once more, and wonders whether it is just him, or if everybody has these strange preferences. Of course everybody, otherwise why would the liberated hippie ask him to do it in the first place? It must be a well-known *phe-no-me-non.* This time he manages to sneak it in. Is it Latin or is it Greek?

"Good. It is perhaps time for you to do things differently. Would you like to give it a try?"

It is when he hears this that the first intimations of the pleasure of a small victory appear at the periphery of Don's awareness. Yes, he could try doing things differently. All kinds of things. Small things and big things. His life was always too constricted, too prescribed, and where has it led him? Like a small child learning to walk he has to be taught to intertwine his fingers. No, that is not the right analogy since after all a small child never knew how to walk. His case is that of a person injured in an accident having to learn for the second time from scratch. The accident is right, but the idea still isn't. He knows how to sit and walk and talk, but never enjoys the freedom of action. Yes, that's it. Everything is pressed upon him by the sheer force of habit. What he needs is to be liberated from his own habits.

"Yes, Doctor." Again, he uses this word. "If it isn't too late to try."

"Oh, no, it is never too late to try. As a matter of fact, you have started already. You see, Don—can I call you Don?" He pushes his chair just a touch closer, and waits for the inevitable nod of ascent—*the salesman of intimacy,* thought Don, *is about to make his pitch.* The nod obediently delivered, he immediately proceeds, without yet offering the reciprocity of Irv, or even Irving. "It is easier to start with the simplest actions, like folding your hands, or arranging your pillow, or shaving, but we should never underestimate their cumulative power over our lives."

Although well aware that these are important things to consider, Don simply can't let a word like cumulative go by. He feels like a predator stalking for words that he can tear to pieces. And it is all carried out in the total privacy of his brain. Nobody, not Dorothy, not Claire, not even this smart Dr. Hunt, has the slightest idea of the drama taking place in front of their noses. *Quite an achievement,* thought Don with a touch of pride. He alone among people can be considered some kind of a *logovore.*

Later, just before leaving his office at the end of their first session, he is given homework. After finding out that Don always shaves his right cheek first, he asks him to reverse the order tomorrow morning and start mixing them up. He is so relieved that the request has nothing to do with his thoughts and fantasies, that he leaves the elephant room in long strides, boldly facing the cold New York evening.

✶✶✶✶✶

Coming out of the hot shower to shave, he enjoys the intense though somewhat futile fight with the steam covering the bathroom mirror. It pits him, with all the resourcefulness of human intelligence, against the physical laws of nature. Each time he wipes the mirror with his hand, his face appears briefly, surrounded by newly formed drops of water. He barely manages to cover his chin with shaving foam before the face is gone. For a while he can still envisage its contours, but soon the vapor makes even that impossible. Fighting back, he wipes the mirror again. This time the quality of the resulting picture is less satisfactory, although it lasts a bit longer.

What a fascinating tradeoff, he thought, as he presses his point with growing obstinacy. He knows that he can open the bathroom door, but that would be cheating, and besides, it's cold outside. He has learned to keep the edges of the mirror in reserve for the final touches to his whiskers. That calls for precision and requires a clear view. When the time comes, he wipes those special areas for the first time, and is often rewarded with a representation of good resolution. Sometimes, in spite of his meticulous planning, the picture is blurred, and true to his resolve, he prefers to risk it rather than look elsewhere. This duel, or rather dance, with the elusive and surprisingly aggressive steam, takes place every single morning and sets the tone for the day ahead.

It is its absence more than anything else that gives him an odd feeling when he spends the night in a hotel, and in the morning he enjoys the unobstructed field of vision provided by a vent and a huge mirror. There is something unsettling about the clarity and the ease of the exercise. He suspects that it is his occasional inclination toward the Spartan that is to blame.

His odd system of shaving developed several years ago, following a particularly nasty backache. Stooping down toward the faucet to wet his face became a tricky business, and there was no way to accomplish it standing upright. Then, one day, he discovered the usefulness of a brief hot shower in preparation for a good smooth shave. However, that precluded drying himself, so he had to stand dripping wet in front of the mirror. The stylized duel with the steam developed later.

All of this could have been easily avoided by resorting to an electric shaver, but he wouldn't hear of it. There is no substitute for a close shave with a sharp razor. Several times a week he cuts himself, usually on his right cheek. He tries to calculate the number of cuts he has sustained over the years and comes up with a number close to eight thousand. He sees his right cheek covered with eight thousand cuts, all bleeding simultaneously.

This is the point the banks are trying to hammer into young people's heads. By starting early and putting aside a small sum toward retirement, over the years they will save an unbelievably huge amount of money. Nest eggs, they call them. But when you are young you don't want to think about old age. You don't think of ever growing old and lonely and sick.

Don realizes that he is approaching treacherous ground and, still dripping, turns to doing his homework. His shaving ritual is quite complicated already, and having to on top of it change the established order of things calls for a major commitment of attention.

Today is Wednesday, and he is starting with the left side. Tomorrow he will go right, and back to the left again on Friday. He should keep a score of this so as not to get mixed up. Don feels anxious and wonders how to make sure that once out of the bathroom he will remember to jot these things down. He feels tense and cuts himself below the chin. He knows that he is doing something wrong, but can't figure out what. It is only when the fight with the steam becomes particularly nasty that it comes to him. His instructions are to mix it up, not to alternate the days. But how can he mix things up? What is mixing up, anyway? No order at all? By what system could he ensure that there wouldn't be any order? No, that is impossible. That is asking too much of him. Anyway, he is the last person in the world to be able to let go of order.

And so it happens that already on this very first day of doing his homework Don has the insight that putting order to everything is his major *modus operandi*. Here is another great Latin expression. So precise. Yes, every single moment of his life is dedicated to fighting chaos. It is as if he were some kind of guardian of order that panics at the slightest hint of things getting out of line. Why panic? What is he scared of? Of change? Of a little spontaneity? Of freedom itself?

By now Don is too excited to care about cutting himself, and as he got back into the shower it dawned on him that his therapist must have known all along what he was doing. And yet it sounded like an entirely harmless exercise. *Smaaaart. Veeeery smart.*

*****

It was only a few weeks into his therapy that the idea of going to Africa surfaced for the first time. That is, if you exclude the elephants, and the many African stories that Irv tells at every possible opportunity. It is as if he were hungry to tell them, and he jumped at every conceivable opportunity to do so. Don likes the stories; at least most of them, and his therapist's eagerness gives him a feeling that their sessions are unique. After all, if he told those stories all the time, the urgency would have gone out of them long ago. At first, Don was taken aback by Irv's obvious attempt to use his patient's time for his own purposes. After a particularly long story Don couldn't help himself and calculated the amount of money he had just paid for the pleasure of listening. That wasn't what they were supposed to be doing.

And yet, there is something about these stories that has a strangely soothing effect on him. They are so full of action and excitement, and his therapist is a good storyteller. Once he starts, Don's attention is totally engaged, with little or no room for the crazy dance of his thoughts. *Maybe that's why he is doing this,* thought Don, *so that I can't go on dissecting everything in my mind.* After the initial exercises with the folding of hands and shaving, and a few others that were similar, he knew that his "coach" was no fool, and that something important was happening to him. He likes to think of him as his personal coach. His trainer in life.

Don's greatest shock, Claire excluded, of course, came on the day when Irv asked him to tell a story of his own. He was in fact talking about Claire, trying to understand whether she was having some type of a midlife crisis, and whether midlife crises were a true phenomenon or purely a convenient stereotype. He preferred the crises explanation to his debacle, and Irv made sure to confront him with his motive.

"I understand that I am biased, but that doesn't mean that I am wrong."

"That is correct," replies his coach, "but can't you accept the fact the adults reach a point where they crave some adventure in their lives? Once the children are out of the house it's easy to think that nothing major is ever going to happen again, and that can be quite frightening, believe me."

Don wonders whether this is spoken from the experience of a therapist or something more personal. It suddenly occurs to him that he knows nothing about Irv's life. There is something disturbing about the asymmetry, but the inevitable question cuts short his line of thought.

"Don't you crave adventure? Or did you have enough adventure in your life already?" And after what appears to be an unusually long silence he goes on to ask his patient to tell him about his adventures. Just one would be enough. Any one.

But hard as he tries, Don can't think of anything that would count as an adventure. *How ridiculous,* he thought, *for a man my age... absolutely ridiculous.*

Like a true hunter, Irving Hunt doesn't make things easier for him and patiently waits in silence. He would do this to him at the worst possible moments, and it is usually quite awkward. But this time it is pure torture, because the longer he searches his brain for something, anything, to tell him, the clearer it becomes that he isn't going to find anything. On top of that, he knows that the longer the silence stretches, the more dramatic the eventual story has to be. However, on this particular occasion it isn't the social inconvenience of silence that he cares about—after all, he is a seasoned patient by now—but rather its origins. Suddenly it all becomes crystal clear: He can't speak of an adventure in his life because he has never had a life to speak of. It is all empty and wasted. What does he have to show for his fifty-two years? Nothing, absolutely nothing, not even a story to tell. Even the emergency landing on their way to the Caribbean vacation turned out to be a false alarm. And when David was three and got lost in the mall it had been scary, but after ten minutes they found him spellbound by the movement of a mobile sculpture, totally unaware of having been lost. No, no adventure there either.

"My only adventure, my only real adventure, was Claire leaving, but you've already heard that story many times."

Don is relieved that it is finally over, while at the same time acutely aware that it is not, that in fact it is only just starting, and that he will have to face this for many an evening over and over again. Should he be glad that Claire had given him a story to tell? Who needs adventures, anyway? But not being able to talk, nay, even to think about one's life, that's a different matter. *It's not the adventure part of it that's important,* he thought, *but rather the absence of any real memories.* Memories of events that are at least minimally interesting. Memories that have a plot. Not just some disjointed pictures in one's mind but stories with a beginning, a middle, and an end.

"You need some adventure in your life," says his coach. "It will do you a lot of good...perhaps take a trip to an interesting place... perhaps you should go to Africa."

That was when his journey to Sinamatella had started. That was when for the first time in a long while he felt the weak intimations of what if properly cultivated might yet develop into a mild hunger for life.

✳✳✳✳✳

Irv sits at his desk trying to collect his thoughts before putting them on paper. He knows how quickly one forgets the details, and for someone in his profession the claim that "God is in the details" certainly makes a lot of sense. It is primarily for this reason that he makes it his rule, at the end of each day, to take some time for reflection and write down whatever he finds useful. For in spite of what might be superficially viewed as a purely intuitive approach, Dr. Irving Hunt's therapeutic work is very methodical. Sometimes he wishes to collect his thoughts at the end of a long day by taking a stroll through the cold Vienna streets like Freud used to do, but the New York version has too many crossings, too many distractions, and besides, he has no daughter to take along. He often wishes he had one, and wonders whether he would have made a good father. It is amazing how many of his patients are totally alienated from their children. This is mostly because they can't handle some stupid adolescent rebellion, or because they are too busy with their careers, or making money. He has to admit, however, that in Don's case the reasons are entirely different.

When he first saw him he was surprised by the immediate outpour of emotion, but shortly afterwards he appeared to settle into the mold that matched Claire's description. "There is no life in him," was her favorite phrase. Today's session certainly proves her right. But where does this lack of *élan vital* (Irv has liked this expression since the very first time he came across it years ago) come from? Surely, despite its early origin it is not systemic. Irv is convinced that it is all defense, and that underneath the thick layer of law and order there is a great deal of hidden volcanic activity.

Take his odd obsession with cutting words into pieces. When Don first confessed his "most private secret," introducing himself as "the one and only logovore on earth," Irv was quick to realize the importance his patient placed in searching for the midpoint of each word. He sees it as an attempt to preserve symmetry and order at all cost. But there is also an element of pride in being the one and only logovore on earth. And aggression too, cutting the words into meaningless pieces and swallowing them. After all he doesn't need to use the word *logovore*. *Homo symmetricus* would be as good, and more accurate.

Irv likes this new expression and starts writing:

March 6. Don as Homo symmetricus. *Perhaps that is why he likes the exercises with the hands and with the shaving so much; they are attempts at symmetry. Words cut into pieces lose much of their meaning. It is impossible to think about their meaning while cutting and counting and dividing by three and zeroing in on the center.* Logos dysinfectus.

A quest for life without bacilli, without smells, without strong colors… without emotion. He is rarely angry, rarely afraid, rarely anything. "There is no life in him," like there was none in Karen Blixen prior to her African venture. Is that why I sent him there?

Africa as a sensory shock treatment. To unfreeze the crust that like an ice cap covers the volcano within. And as an afterthought, he added:

But even if it works, it would be just the first step.

Intimacy

Back from his trip down memory lane, his limbs stiff from the unchanged posture conducive to prolonged reminiscence, Don knows that eventually he will have to stop procrastinating and write about the long African night following the encounter with the lions. There is something that prevented him from doing so just yet, as if prior to sharing them he wants to dwell on those events in the protected state of his loneliness. It is a mixture of pleasant secrecy combined with worries about his capacity to be entirely honest in writing about what happened. He knows it for a sign of weakness on his part, but as it has only been one week since he came to Sinamatella he shouldn't be too hard on himself.

Many things concerning that night fascinate him, but it is the mind/body problem presented in all its nakedness that intrigues him most. Although Irv often talks about the psychosomatic route, particularly when trying to explain to him the constant feeling of fatigue, this is of an entirely different order of magnitude. Don laughs at the way his mind insists on coming up with expressions with double meanings. It is as if his unconscious is trying to hint at something, systematically forcing him to seriously consider what happened. Only this time it isn't by the usual brutal invasion of his thoughts, but through subtlety and humor. He likes it, and thinks that it may indicate something good.

He feels excited, almost happy, that entire afternoon, without knowing why. It is a new feeling and he cherishes the awareness of well-being that permeates his body. Every movement that he makes is just right, and he feels as if he's recovering from a long illness. When evening comes, and they all sit around the fire sipping coffee, Don feels less inhibited than usual and engages the others in lively conversation. True, all is not smooth, and right in the middle of telling the story of the emergency landing en route to the Caribbean, he suddenly feels guilty for not mentioning Claire, as though she doesn't exist, and cuts his story short. *I got carried away,* he thought. *Drunk on the lions.*

To the right, at the periphery of his field of vision, he is aware of Iris's watchful eyes. It is a constant presence that he dares not check too often. And yet, each time he turns his head slightly to bring her more into focus, she is there, and he isn't sure anymore whether his feeling light-headed has anything to do with the lions.

This feeling of slight intoxication is so new to him that he doesn't know what to do with it. During a break in the general conversation he is drawn into self-observation, and from the vantage point of detachment finds himself quite ridiculous. This brief but obviously dangerous pause is cut short by another log being put on the fire, and for a while Don feels saved from the tyranny of his thoughts.

"You think too much," is what Irv had said to him more than once. "You think too much for your own good. Just like Hamlet."

Don knows that it's true, but can't think of anything that might stop him. Now the fire does it for him. And the stars. And the warm coffee. And the young woman sitting not too far from him to his right.

The conversation turns to the events of the morning, and Mike, who missed the whole thing, is trying to gain entry by asking questions that are so general that the details of the experience become less important.

"What was it about the morning that you liked best?" And later, "Were you afraid when the lioness charged?"

Don listens to what they say with great interest, all the time feeling the tension building in his chest. "Just briefly," one person says. "Not really," says another, "but the rifle shot gave me a fright."

"I don't know about you," Don hears himself saying, "but for a while I was in a state of shock. It was like being terrified and spellbound simultaneously…it wasn't like the fear was unpleasant. On the contrary, there was something very exciting and tempting about it." And after a short pause during which he sensed that everyone was waiting for him to continue, he said, "It was a perfect time to die."

He doesn't know what has come over him, but the tension is now gone, and he feels relieved. The tone of his last words made it obvious that he doesn't intend to say anything more, but neither do the others. The long silence is broken only by the occasional crackling of the fire, and the strange sounds of the African bush. And in that silence, which to his own surprise he has forced upon them, sensing the power emanating from him in all directions but particularly to the right, Don feels young and happy.

Consequently, after some moments when he sees Iris quietly getting up and leaving for her tent, he isn't just disappointed, but genuinely sad, as if something precious that was briefly found has been lost again, perhaps forever.

Hours later, in his tent, he hears her soft footsteps long before she pauses at the entrance to whisper his name, which has suddenly became a password to their night together.

Don has since been reconstructing this part thousands of times, and even now, in his room in Sinamatella, he tries to evoke those footsteps and that soft voice whispering, "Don," and the impatient, almost aggressive way in which he unzipped, nay, tore open the flaps of the tent, and her, crouching down onto all fours to squeeze through the entrance, and him, noticing the thousands of bright stars like a halo around her head, thinking that she might not be wearing anything under her loose, extra-extra-large sweatshirt, in such marked contrast with her tight shirt of morning fame.

At first he doesn't know what to do with his hands, but then they find her full breasts, hanging loose and heavy under her sweatshirt....

The abundance of her, the hard breathing, and the long kisses carried out almost to the point of suffocation, him clinging to her open mouth like a drowning man receiving resuscitation, not a word spoken, only internally, *Oh, you came, you came,* not sure whether this is spoken or only thought, and then:

"What you said there, near the fire, was the most beautiful thing I have ever heard."

Don wonders whether her passion is an outburst of the spirit or of the flesh. He can engage that mystery now, but at the time it had taken place he just felt enormous pride, mixed with a touch of shame, as if he had been caught cheating. That might have been the problem, but mostly he thinks that their eagerness is to blame. The eagerness and the impatience intensified by his disappointment preceding this bliss.

It is all hurried, and he thinks that he isn't ready…and later he realizes that in spite of his boundless desire for this young woman who suddenly entered his dreary life, he isn't ever going to be ready, at least not that night.

"I can do things that will help…do you want me to?"

Don wants it very much; oh, how he wants her to do things to him. Things that Claire never did and that he had read about, but now he is too scared and worried that they won't work, so he says, "No, there is no need. Don't bother."

"It's not for me," says Iris. "It isn't so important to me, but I thought that you'd feel better…you know."

But too many words have been said by now, and like an invisible barrier they occupy the space between them, and the opportunity is lost.

Imp-ot-ent. From the vantage point of hindsight Don allows himself the luxury of engaging in his old habits without worrying about it too much, although he isn't sure how to feel. Don recalls reading something about how Goethe travels on his own and tries to seduce a beautiful innkeeper, then finds himself impotent. He goes to his room and writes a love letter to his wife, confessing the fiasco that he interpreted as a sign of his love for her. Don can't remember where he read it, but now it comes to him very vividly, and he wonders about its meaning. Can it be that he still loves Claire? Should he write her a letter?

After several attempts they give up, and lying on his back, her head on his chest, her abundant hair now wild and free and almost touching his nose, Don inhales her smell and slowly relaxes. He unzips the flaps of the small tent to let the starlight in, and the sounds and sights of the African night slowly push carnal disappointment into the background. They can hear the distant roar of a lion, followed by the diminishing volume of his grunts. A zebra barks furiously, a dangerous thing to do at night. Then he hears the unmistakable bloodcurdling laughter of hyenas. There must be several of them; the sound is both frightening and exciting at the same time.

"What brought you to Africa?"

It is a natural question to ask and yet Don hesitates for a while before answering. The honesty of his reply, "I was hurting and came to heal," gives him an odd sense of freedom, and after a brief silence he goes on: "My wife left me, and I was a total wreck. I became preoccupied with suicidal thoughts and consulted a psychologist. It was he who suggested that Africa would do me a lot of good."

He feels no inhibition in telling Iris about himself, as if his masculine failure left no room for pretense. She asks a lot of questions about the children, particularly about Naomi, which he answers rather curtly. He feels guilty for not writing to her yet. It strikes him as odd that it has taken so little time to tell her everything that she wants to know, and everything that he considers worth saying. By the time he is done there is hardly any visible change in the position of the stars. He thinks that he should mention this to Irv. It is a sobering revelation. Then he asks her about her own life.

She is a student—barely older than Naomi—about to take her final exams in the fall. Irvine, California. Joint geography and anthropology program. Don thinks that this is the connection to

Africa, but he is wrong. It is a promise she made to Julie, her closest friend, before the brain tumor killed her.

There is a pause in her story, and Don can hear the tremor in her voice. He gently strokes her endlessly long hair, waiting for her to go on.

"Julie and I were inseparable. She was the gentlest person I ever met, and the best of friends. We had known each other since junior high and did everything together. Hiking, biking, even whitewater canoeing. She was physically tough, always trying to outdo the boys on their turf. So gentle, and...so romantic at the same time."

The unmistakable laugh of a hyena. Then just the croaks of frogs from a nearby pool. Don is very much with her, seeing her biking vigorously, her healthy young body deeply tanned, California style. It is a scene of laughter and freedom, something that he knew existed, but unlike anything found in his own restricted Jewish urban adolescence.

"We had this fetish about Africa. We devoured Hemingway and read the diaries of Livingstone, and Stanley, and Baker of the Nile, and, of course, Burton and Speke. Africa was our common secret. We loved everything about it and spent long weekends planning our first safari. It should have been our graduation present to ourselves. Something that we owed to our friendship before life sent us and our future families in different directions."

She is leaning against him, her breasts pressed close. Her head rests on his chest, and as she talks the movement of her lips and larynx sends soft waves across his body. Her hair smells of shampoo, and when inhaling deeply it tickles his nostrils. His left hand continues to stroke her head, while his right follows the sloping curve of her waist and thighs. He takes great care not to change the rhythm of his caress, hoping it will be accepted as a natural part of the situation.

"Five months ago they found the tumor; it was the size of a small grapefruit." She pauses again, as if realizing that such an image should be granted some time to fully manifest itself. Don recalls that right there, in his tent, with his hands all the while stealthily exploring Iris's body, the *grapefruit* was particularly disturbing.

"It was awful. Shortly after surgery was attempted Julie lost consciousness for long periods of time. When she came to she was confused and mostly didn't recognize me. Then during one of her rare lucid moments, shortly before she died, she made me promise to go to Africa for both of us. This very summer, she insisted. Don't postpone it, please! Don't postpone anything! Ever."

✶✶✶✶✶

In spite of her promise he isn't sure whether she will come the following night. At some point during the long wait he tries to ready himself for her, but even though it helps for a while, it is too technical, and he can't trust it. He knows that worrying about it will only make things worse but can't help himself. *If I knew how to do that, I wouldn't need my shrink,* he thought, and as evening gave way to night he slowly accepts his fate. *Come what may,* he tells himself, without noticing the pun, at times almost hoping she won't come.

But she does, and by the starlight at the entrance to his tent he sees that her hair is different. Instead of the carefree, long—*and young,* he thinks—looseness, it is pulled back tightly and into a single thick ponytail. The tightness makes her face that of a mature woman, and her ponytail that of a girl.

Their initial kissing and groping is almost as wild as on the first night, and in the midst of his intoxication Don catches himself thinking that everything is doomed to repeat itself. But somewhere down the enchanted road, and in spite of subsequently trying hard, Don can't pinpoint the exact moment, they seem to flow into a gentle stream that urges them on and at the same time carries them on deeper and deeper, smoothly, without obstacles, no words exchanged, her soft moaning and his hard breathing playing the duet of their lovemaking. He feels as strong as the lion from yesterday, and when the crescendo comes, his grunts sound like a mild version of the original.

Three times during the long African night Don rises to the occasion, and in the morning, spent and enmeshed in the warmth and smells that Iris left behind, he feels vigorous and happy. The questions come only later, and joining Mike and the others near the fire for a cup of early morning coffee, they are not yet even at the periphery of his awareness.

Even now, as he is playing these events over in his mind for the hundredth time, he knows that writing Irv about them will be a complicated affair. During his stay in Sinamatella he has composed several versions of the opening lines in his head, and the more lines he writes, the more difficult it will be to pick the right one. He likes the shocking one best:

Dear Irv,

So you managed to wake up my libido, but what good is it to me? First it gets me all crazy about this young blond from California, and then it dies on me with her in my arms. Next it fills me with the virility of a lion, and shortly after turns into a pool of guilt.

What he likes about this one is its economy. It says so much in just a few sentences. But then Irv will have no idea what he is writing about.

Dear Irv,

It's no use. I still love Claire, and I still hurt hopelessly. The proof? My impotence with the greatest conquest of my life. See Goethe's letter to his wife.

Or:

Dear Irv,

Happiness is a trap. Its sole purpose is to make the subsequent misery more potent. Stay away from it. And sexual happiness is the worst of the lot. Neither past nor future in it, only the present. (You undoubtedly wonder where my expertise suddenly came from. Just wait until you hear my story.) When you sent me on this African adventure, did you seriously believe that the present would cure me of the past? Or that at my age I would be content with the here and now?

Don likes this one as well, although he isn't sure what exactly he means by it all. However, is sounds just about right. He knows that it is possible to start with the questions and tell the story later, although there is something fundamentally unfair about it. Like pretending to know the future. Or like giving an interpretation of an earlier event from the vantage point of hindsight. Isn't this precisely what Irv has been doing all along? Smart after the event. *Some of the questions are legitimate in their own right, irrespective of the story that precedes them,* he thinks. *Risk taking for one.*

Dear Irv,

I had unprotected sex with an obviously sexually active partner. It was unquestionably the best experience I have ever had, and at no point during the long night did the question of AIDS or a condom cross my mind. (But rest assured that I am paying for it now. With interest.) Totally spontaneous, totally absorbing. No room for doubts or even THOUGHTS. Imagine, Irv, NO ROOM FOR THOUGHTS. And remember, this is your obsessive-compulsive Don Mendelson reporting.

He likes the "reporting," and toys with the idea of signing off (in the best reporters' language) with "this is Don Mendelson reporting from Sinamatella." Reminds him of CNN. Reminds him of the world. Of his office. Of the life he left momentarily in pursuit of some mysterious inner calling.

Yes, Don Mendelson, accept the fact that you of all people are suddenly emerging as a gambler. Taking risks with your established career, taking huge economic risks, and on top of it all even health risks. Imagine returning to New York HIV positive. Viruses are truly cosmopolitan, he thought. From California to New York via Zimbabwe. He knows that he is being extremely unfair to Iris, his beautiful Iris whom he misses desperately, but the thought just won't go away. He should try to get himself tested in Harare, or better still in Bulawayo. A long day's journey from Sinamatella. He can surely get a lift to Bulawayo on one of the minibuses touring the National Park. That will also give him a chance to call Dorothy, and perhaps Naomi or David. And he can rent a car and come right back. More mobile that way, with the option of making a few game drives on his own in addition to just sitting at the top and watching from above.

Don has a Castle beer at the small bar, and asks the barman to help him arrange a lift to Bulawayo. Big man, with a long red and white beard (*compensating for being almost totally bald,* thought Don), pink face, green eyes, and were it not for the distinctive Afrikaans accent he could pass for Irish.

"Leaving us, eh?"

"Just for a few days."

"So you'll be coming back to us, eh?"

"Yes."

Don is not a frequent visitor to the bar, but he realizes that his presence in Sinamatella must have been the topic of local gossip. After all, they all know that originally he had come as part of a group of Americans, and for some reason he has stayed behind. Alone. Without a car. Strange person, always brooding, always distant.

"Name is Ian," he said, extending his hand, his gentle smile in marked contrast to the rough voice.

"Don."

"Pleasure."

And so begins a long conversation. After the perfunctory remarks about the beauty of the place and the richness of its wildlife it quickly turns into more of an interrogation, with Ian asking the questions and Don giving short answers. Then Ian provides two more Castles and joins him in having a drink. It isn't long before Ian asks him whether he was disgusted with the others in the group.

"Myself, I could never travel with so many people. Gets on my nerves."

"It wasn't so bad, but I wanted to have some time to myself."

Ian likes the answer, and after a pause pours both of them some more beer, and lifts his glass for a toast.

"Here's to the joys of loneliness."

"Cheers," says Don, unable to come up with anything more profound. It has been almost a full week since he has talked with anyone, and he feels some basic camaraderie with this person exulting the virtues of loneliness. *What a paradox,* he thought. *Loners of the world unite!* His second Castle almost gone, he suddenly wishes that Claire hadn't left just like that. He feels abandoned and sad.

"The next round is on me," he says.

Ian opens two more ice-cold bottles and pours for both of them, making sure that each drinks from his own bottle. *He must be a very private person.* Don wonders what tale brought him to this remote part of the world. *Everybody has a story. Well, perhaps not everybody, but many do.* He realizes that he never suspected it. The same way that he never suspected Claire. At the age of fifty-two he feels himself to be as naïve as a child. All his life has been an illusion. Even Iris knows more about certain things than he does. Like what being at the deathbed of your closest friend around the clock does to you. Or how to make love. Yes, definitely a sexually active woman.

When Ian tries to explore his motives further, Don can't say much, realizing that he himself has only a vague idea about them. The last night in Sinamatella the group had a discussion about the trip, and what it had meant for each one of them so far. It was then that Don suddenly had the urge to shock them all (the previous occasion being such a big success) and without having thought it through properly announced his intention to stay. He could see the surprise on Iris's face quickly change to anger. Why hadn't he told her? Was he trying to run away from her? The first to speak was Mike, saying that he didn't think it was possible. After all, participation in the group entailed a contractual agreement, and he was responsible for bringing all of them home safely. Envy? The young bull suddenly threatened by the old one? It was bullshit, and after Don promised to provide him with a clear declaration of his wishes, releasing him from all responsibility, it was settled.

Later, in his room, he hoped she would come, giving him a chance to explain. It had nothing to do with her, he would say. Nothing at all. On the contrary, she had given him the strength to make the decision. He needed to be alone and clear his mind about certain things. It was impossible to do it in New York. And what better place than Sinamatella? When they first climbed the hill and looked at the vast expanse reaching all the way to Kalahari he was physically affected by it. Yes, he would describe to her the sudden feeling of freedom that he had experienced.

But Iris was sulking and didn't come. Maybe it was just as well, for by now he was worried about AIDS, and not having access to a condom couldn't see himself asking questions and making excuses in the middle of their lovemaking. It was a long night, and he was slowly realizing the meaning of what he had done. The wish to shock them all was childish. "Infantile," Irv would undoubtedly call it. He also sensed that Iris was right and that to some extent he was running away from her. The last three days had been scary in their intensity, and with all the unfinished business between him and Claire he wasn't yet ready for something like this. Free of Claire, slave to Iris. There was also, he knew, the fear of losing her once they left the African bush and found themselves in more ordinary circumstances. Without the evening fire, and the lions, and the stars of the African night, he didn't stand a chance with a beautiful woman who could be his daughter. There was enough time during that long night to wonder whether he hadn't decided to stay just to impress her? To impress Irv? To impress himself? As the night started to give way to dawn he tried to cut his losses. *It is only for a few days, at most a week,* he thought. *No harm done. And in any event, after the theatrical announcement there was no way back. A gambler indeed.*

But he can't tell Ian any of this and in spite of the Castle loosening his tongue he manages to avoid his probing questions. Instead, he asks him about Bulawayo.

"You should visit Matopos."

"Is it really that special?"

"Nothing like it."

Don knows that it is the last stop on his group's itinerary before flying back, and he had seen the strange rock formations prominently featured on the tourist brochures, but that is all.

Now Ian is getting visibly excited. "Speaking of loneliness, there is no place like Matopos for loneliness. Even Cecil Rhodes knew that when he chose the spot for his grave. Worth seeing. Definitely."

Don makes a mental note of the recommendation, and proceeds to ask about the town itself, how modern it is, and what types of facilities it has. He doesn't want to ask directly about a hospital or a clinic, or whether there are some European physicians left. He knows that Sinamatella or not, with his obsessive nature he will know no peace until he gets tested for HIV, but the question is whether it will be safe to take the test. By now Ian had become very quiet and moody, and Don decides that he will see for himself before deciding one way or another.

The next morning, shortly after his usual breakfast of cereal and scrambled eggs on the verandah overlooking the park, he boards one of the minibuses leaving for Bulawayo. Seven tourists from Germany, their guide, and the driver. They are noisily comparing their notes about their photographic experiences, and he is glad to sit in the back avoiding conversation. For some time he tries to find the center of the word *Bulawayo,* and it bothers him because he isn't sure whether it is spelled with a single *l* or with two *l*s. The difference for his task is, of course, enormous. He even toys with the idea of having it both ways, alternating Irv style. Mondays, Wednesday, Fridays with a single *l*, and Tuesdays, Thursday, Saturdays with two. On Sundays people should be free to use either. They make a stopover for lunch at the Gwaai River Hotel, a typical Victorian place that has known better days, and he finds himself sitting with the guide and an elderly couple who keep showing him the map on which they have marked all the places they have visited. They speak English with a very strong German accent, ending most of their sentences with a "*ja*" that sounds like a question. "Tomorrow we visit the Matopos, *ja*? Zen we visit the Highlands, *ja*?" Don manages to steal a glance at their map to find out the correct spelling of Bulawayo. He is glad when it is over, and as the sun is setting they enter the city. It starts to drizzle and it is cold. He leaves the bus at what appears to him to be the main street, and for the first time in who knows how many years, he finds himself alone in a totally strange place. It is not an unpleasant feeling; there is something exciting about it.

Alighting from the bus without any luggage, some money, his credit cards, and his toothbrush the only things he has on him, he feels light and free. The street is busy with shoppers. The telephones are situated at the main post office, but it's already closed and will have to wait for tomorrow. He needs a place to stay but doesn't want to go to the same hotel as his lunch partners, which he understands is "very good, *ja*?"

He stumbles on the local information office, and the old lady there greets him with a pleasant smile and makes a few phone calls for him, arranging his accommodation at a nice and quiet place within walking distance. "Hello, Marigold, this is Jane from the tourist bureau," she says, stressing the *bureau*, and Don envies the obvious familiarity and feeling of being at home she must have. As a New Yorker, that is something he has never experienced. His parents used to talk about the "good old times" when there was still a sense of community in their Brooklyn neighborhood, but he and Claire and most of their friends looked down on such symptoms of provincialism befitting a small Midwestern town and not the great cosmopolitan metropolis. Bulawayo isn't New York, and the number of white residents must be quite small, and they probably meet in the local Rotary or Lions and play bridge Thursday nights and tombola every other Saturday. But the sting of envy is there just the same, and he feels lonelier.

The place was farther than he expected, and by the time he gets there he is wet and cold. After Marigold gets him settled in the room he finds that the warmest place is at the bar, which is filled with people and smoke. He gets himself a Castle and finding a safe position in the corner looks around. It is good to see both white and black customers sitting together. *Zimbabwe must be doing something right*, he thought. Clearly only a few people are staying at the hotel, indicating that the bar is popular with the locals.

"Can I join you?" This from a tall dark man with long braids of curly black hair dangling on either side of a face with some oriental touch. A hint of high cheekbones, the sparking, intelligent eyes just a little slanted.

"Please. Take a seat." Don has no choice in the matter despite a feeling of apprehension. There is something unsettling about this intruder; perhaps the long braids are too New York hippie for his tastes. At first he even thinks that he might be an African American, but the accent doesn't fit.

"American?"

"Yes," says Don, slightly embarrassed by how obvious it is.

"Passing through?"

"Yes, you could say that."

"Have you been to Matopos yet?"

What is all this about Matopos, thought Don. *Is there no other topic of conversation at a bar?* "No. I've only just arrived."

"But you will go there before leaving." This was more of a statement than a question. It appears that his companion wouldn't consider anything else. He wouldn't share a drink with someone who would skip Matopos.

"I'll try."

"If you want, I can take you there." The eyes shining, the face eager. Don can't decide whether this person is trying to sell him his services, or whether he is genuinely offering to be his personal guide. The uneasy feeling will not leave him, and he recognizes a need for caution. But before he can think of what to say, his partner's enthusiasm sweeps all his misgivings aside. "I can show you the real Matopos, not the usual touristy place. It would be my pleasure." He moves his chair closer to the table, leaning across, all fired up. "Can I buy you another Castle?"

"Thanks, but I'm doing fine." Don is thankful for the opportunity to answer the second question and dodge the initial offer. He is struck by the fact that it's so easy to start a conversation with a total stranger. Yesterday Ian the barman, and now this person. This is new to him, and he doesn't know what to make of it.

"I'm Don," he says, taking the initiative.

"My name is Jordan, but friends call me Mwewe." His handshake is firm, but the texture of his hand is rough and wrinkled. *Probably older than I am,* Don thought. *Could be my age.*

"Tell me, Mwewe—can I call you Mwewe?"

"You must."

"What is it about Matopos that makes people's eyes shine?"

"I like the way you talk, Don. Let me tell you, now that place has mystery." And after a short pause he continues, obviously excited. "Are you a man of mystery?"

"I don't know what you mean. I have no idea if I'm a man of mystery or not. I think that for most of my life I haven't been, but lately I'm not so sure anymore."

"You either are a man of mystery or you are not. You cannot change it. It is something deep inside you, probably from birth. I like men of mystery. I am such a man myself. Very much so."

Don tries to think who among his acquaintances could pass for a man of mystery, but he can't think of a single one. He thinks about Irv, but he is too sophisticated and too smart for that. Perhaps his old philosophy teacher in college. He can't recall his name, but there was something unworldly, and yes, mysterious, about that man. He used to say things that nobody understood. He talked as if reciting lines of poetry and his gaze was always unfocused, misty. Is mystery related to mist? No, this area certainly isn't his forte. After all, naïve and blind as he has been it was only recently that he started his own initiation into the mysteries of life.

"Tell me about yourself," Don says. "I want to learn what men of mystery are like." By now Don feels dry and pleasantly warm, and his initial reservations about this unbidden intruder are quickly turning into outright curiosity. They order a couple of beers and as Mwewe starts to unfold his tale their small table in the corner becomes an island isolated not only from the rest of the people crowding the bar, but from the rest of the world as well.

Mwewe

"My story is the story of Africa," he starts, his voice deep and melodious. "It is a story the likes of which you may hear from many people on this unhappy continent." Don is struck both by the caliber of his English and by the beauty of the narrative. His voice has a hypnotic quality, and before long he is totally under its spell.

"I was raised on the mission, a few miles from the village where my mother and her relatives lived. My father left for the big city shortly after I was born and never came back. My mother told me that he was a very special man, and that the village was too small for him. I never understood what was so special about him, but people who knew him seemed to agree that he had some spiritual gifts and was destined for greatness. But he was never heard of again, and probably died long ago."

Mwewe, who is looking directly into Don's eyes, now seems to change his focus to somewhere in the distance. The loud noise of the bar can suddenly be heard. Don senses the sadness in the man in front of him and patiently waits for him to resume his tale.

"Life on the mission wasn't bad, particularly since my older brother was with me and took care of me. The school on the mission was the only one in the whole area, and all the boys and girls from the village studied there. They had to walk more than one hour each way, and often had to run in order not to miss the morning prayers...do you know why Africans make such good long-distance runners? Most of them had to run every day to school and back. That's why. You can check it out. All our famous athletes started training from grade one. No yellow bus in the bush."

Don can't believe his ears. How in the world did Mwewe know about yellow school buses? He must find out about that. He doesn't want to interrupt with such a banal question, but it sticks in his mind and won't go away. Suddenly he feels excited. He sees the title of a book that he might write some day: *No Yellow Bus in the Bush*. Yes, he must ask him later.

"On cold winter mornings, or when the big rains came, I felt lucky for staying on the mission, although I missed my mother a lot. We were not allowed to leave the premises. The missionary and his wife were kindhearted people, but they insisted on strict discipline. Between school, and work in the garden, and prayers, there was no time for anything else, and we could rarely play. Sometimes mother came for a short visit, and those were the happiest moments of my life...she never came empty-handed, although I couldn't care less about the little presents of food or clothing that she carried in her small straw basket. On these occasions it was always my brother who saw her first. The pastor's wife would send for him, and later he would look for me. I suspected him of delaying as much as possible, so that he could spend some time with Mother alone. While she was there I didn't mind, but immediately after she left I became obsessed with envy. It was then that my ability for clairvoyance was first discovered."

Don is again caught off guard. First the yellow bus, and now this clairvoyance. Is there no end to the surprises that Mwewe has in store for him?

"One morning, in the middle of a reading class, I suddenly knew that Mother was on her way to the mission. It was not just some form of abstract knowledge—I could actually see her walking. I asked permission to go to the bathroom and ran like mad in the direction of the village. After about a mile I was completely exhausted and had to sit under an old acacia tree to catch my breath. Frustrated by my weak body, I was crying when she found me. Since that day I often knew about her coming, and found ways to meet her under that acacia tree. At first she didn't believe me, and worried that I did this practically every day, skipping my classes. She must have asked at the mission, because after some time she seemed to believe me, and said that I was just like my father."

Like a good storyteller, Mwewe stops at this point to allow his audience to appreciate what has been said, and Don takes advantage of the pause. "You said that you often knew about her coming, but apparently not always. What made you know and what prevented you from knowing?"

"Oh, many things. You see, this gift of mine, strange as it sounds, was always well rooted in material reality. Even now, if I eat something that is not good for me, or if I drink too much beer, or if the rains stop, or if I get up in the morning with bad thoughts in my head, I know for sure that on such a day I will never be able to transcend the limited world of the senses. It is as if everything has to be just right...but of course it rarely is."

"So you still have this...this gift of yours?" Don is tempted to say "clairvoyance" just to hear himself pronouncing it, but at the last moment he changes his mind. He is about to search for the midpoint of this wonderfully long and mysterious word, but Mwewe doesn't give him sufficient time.

"Oh yes, I still have it...sometimes. You see, I need it for my work."

"What do you do?"

"I am a geologist—I work for a large German development company that mines precious metals."

"And you tell them where to dig?"

"Sometimes."

Don wonders what this thing about "sometimes" is, but leaves it for future analysis.

"You see," Mwewe continues, "there is no way for them to know whether I picked up a promising location as a trained geologist, or as a man with special powers. I myself often cannot distinguish between them. I would never recommend a spot without being able to document it on the basis of solid argument. But there might be other locations with similar credentials that I would never recommend." Mwewe smiles mischievously, as if enjoying this special secret. "I used to be better when I was much younger...before the war of independence... but not with precious metals. My specialty was finding water. In these parts of Africa there is always a shortage of water. You cannot trust the rains, and most villages depend entirely on digging their own wells."

Don tries to calculate Mwewe's age, and whether he could have been a trained geologist before Zimbabwe's independence, but there are still too many missing details. He shouldn't have cut into the story with his questions. "I'm sorry that I disturbed your tale. Please go on."

"There is not much to tell. After finishing elementary school the missionary insisted that I continue with high school. I was sent to another mission, in town, and finished first in my class. But these were the days of Ian Smith, Rhodesia was reeling under international sanctions, and I couldn't find any work. 'You are overqualified,' they would say, meaning that for hard menial labor they would rather employ someone with as little schooling as possible. I might have ideas about fair wages, and reasonable work hours, and even, God forbid, about race relations. It was then that I started my career as a diviner of water, and after a few initial successes people from nearby villages would ask me to come and try again. I knew that I was lucky with the first ones, and didn't want to test it too often, but then Matabeleland had one of its worst droughts in years, and I had no choice. And so it was that I became quite famous. People started calling me Jordan the Provider, as if my first name had been some kind of prophecy in its own right. Those who knew my father claimed that by choosing to call me Jordan he must have seen into the future. But I was skeptical, and each time I found water I thanked God for my luck. True, there were times when I was quite confident, when I could almost hear the water in my ears, but that was rare. So I had no choice but to learn about water as much as I could. It occurred to me that perhaps I was just picking up some obvious signs in the lay of the land that nobody paid any attention to. I thought that the only thing I had was some special sensitivity, that I could read what the countryside was trying to tell us about what lies hidden beneath the surface. I believed that there must be a perfectly rational explanation to everything. Everything, that is, except for matters relating to my mother. That was on a different level, based on the strong emotional bond between us. But water? Why should there be any mystery about water? So I tried to demystify my own success by closely watching for even the weakest of signs. I would spend hours walking around the village trying to put myself in the water's place. If I were water, which way would I flow? Where would I collect? However, even that sometimes failed me, and I would leave the village amid great disappointment. But the people were so desperate that they still refused to give up their belief in my powers. And then Jordan the Provider would be taken to yet another village, and find water. It was all very confusing."

That doesn't surprise Don, since he is getting more and more confused himself. First there was this thing with his mother, and how it didn't always work, and then the trained geologist tried to combine western scientific method with primitive intuition. And what was this need for luck? And what is luck, anyway? And why of all people would he try to demystify his own success? Trying to put himself in the water's place—it didn't make sense. Is that what being a man of mystery meant? Having had one Castle too many, and sitting in this strange city where he came to find out whether he was mortally ill or not, Don feels that he is too vulnerable to things of mystery. He must be on guard against being unduly impressed by this strange person revealing his life story in such immaculate English. Jordan the Pretender? Mwewe the Con Man? And yet, how rich, how wonderfully rich his story is. How full of beginnings, and middles, and ends. Even a single visit to one of those thirsty villages has more adventure in it than all the years of toiling in his office could ever have.

"Go on, please."

Mwewe seems to be coming back from a long distance, and Don worries that he will not wish to continue his tale in front of this white stranger who isn't giving anything in return. Fortunately he can't know that his audience is so impoverished that it has nothing to give. Well, perhaps that is not exactly true anymore. Don imagines himself telling Mwewe about Claire, and Irv, and the lions, and about Iris. He feels good about this list of things he can tell. Can he tell him about Sinamatella? He isn't sure how one should go about it. Sinamatella is his mystery. His Matopos.

"My life suddenly took a dramatic change. I was approached by representatives of Zanu who wanted me to join them. They said that Joshua Nkomo himself had heard about the youngster who had these special gifts and sent them to recruit me to the national cause. I was flattered, and enthusiastic about fighting for the freedom of my country."

Don isn't sure if what sounds like a touch of cynicism is his own invention or real. Mwewe talks much faster now, as if he were angry, or perhaps wanted to get past this part as quickly as possible.

"I was not allowed to talk to anyone and without saying goodbye to my mother and my brother was taken to the highlands and smuggled across the border to Mozambique. From there I had to be transferred all the way to Tanzania. Mozambique was still a Portuguese colony, and all travel had to be done at night. There were seven of us, and it took us almost a full month to get there. We had no food and no money and had to rely on stealing from poor villagers. On several occasions we were apprehended and barely made it. By the time we finally crossed into Tanzania the rains had started, and we were all sick.

"All ZANU and ZAPU camps were stationed near the Zambian border, and ours was no exception. We were issued green fatigues and started basic training. Much of the training consisted of political indoctrination. While ZANU was under Soviet Marxist influence, its rival ZAPU belonged to the Chinese Maoist camp. I was a good student and excelled in tracking the bush. I enjoyed searching for the "enemy" and could easily orient myself without a compass. We were often left alone in a dense bush and had to find our way back to our base. It was like navigating at sea without a map. It was much easier than navigating the waters below the surface. I was so good at it that instead of Jordan everybody started to call me Seagull—*Mwewe* in Swahili. At the end of the course I was among the few selected to be sent to East Germany for advanced training in guerilla warfare."

Gone is the slow, deep, resonant voice of the storyteller. It has now been irrevocably replaced by the impatient staccato of a participant in an ominous enterprise. While at the time an obviously willing participant, the subsequent harsh judgment of these events doesn't escape Don's notice. He can almost feel it as a physical presence located somewhere in his throat. *Maybe that's why the human voice is such a sensitive indicator of emotion,* he thought. The slightest tension in the music chamber impacts the vocal chords. Each time he plans to say something in public he feels the urge to cough and clear his voice. It was Irv who brought his attention to this. He misses Irv and wishes he were in the noisy bar right now, to share the experience. Mwewe takes a long sip of Castle. To clear his throat? To blunt the memory?

"Life in East Germany was very unpleasant. The training was OK, but the attitude of the locals to us Africans was much worse than anything I ever saw in Rhodesia. I was there for six months and picked up some of the language. The winter was bad—it was always cold. The people were full of hate and they rarely smiled. They hated the West Germans, the Russians, the Americans, the communist party, their awful past, their miserable present, and the absence of any future. I have never seen so much hate. But they were true professionals, and we got the best training possible. From there, it was straight to the Zambia Rhodesia border, and the real thing."

Don knows that the border consists of the mighty Zambezi River of Victoria Falls fame. He tries to picture a young Mwewe, on a moonless night, full of patriotic fervor, crossing the crocodile-infested river on a hit-and-run mission.

"The important thing was not to walk into an ambush. Once you walked into an ambush you were dead. Many of our best fighters never made it. On several occasions I could sense the presence of enemy troops waiting ahead and aborted my mission. It could have been the smell of their fear carried over a long distance. Perhaps it was the deep emotional bond that exists between enemies. There was no way to find out whether my premonition was valid or not, and staying alive was my only proof. Soon some of the comrades preferred to have me as a scout. They thought it would bring them luck, that like a proper seagull I would always find my way back unharmed. I did, and with each successful raid my confidence grew. I thought I was indestructible and was absolutely certain that when there would be a major danger lurking in the darkness I would somehow know about it."

Don has a premonition that he will soon learn about something terrible that happened. He wonders whether he can smell it, hear it, or see it. *Just like Mwewe,* he thought. *Just like Mwewe.*

"It was around this time that my older brother joined our unit. For more than a year now I had been forbidden to maintain any contact with my family, so I was delighted to see him. Our mother was not too well, and most of the young people from our village were either with ZANU or were recruited to help the whites of Rhodesia defend themselves against us. The specter of fighting each other was too frightening to even think about. When my brother heard about my reputation as a scout he couldn't resist telling everybody about the water, and about our father, and before long I found myself burdened by totally unrealistic expectations. Before launching an operation the commanding officer would ask me to tell him which of two possible routes to take. I tried to explain to him that there was no way I could give him that advice. Often, I claimed, I was just lucky, and nothing more. And on the few occasions that I did perhaps have some form of clairvoyance, it was entirely unplanned and uncalled for, and I couldn't possibly evoke it intentionally. The stakes, however, were too great, and try as I did to proclaim my lack of extraordinary powers, nobody seemed to believe me. And all this time I was crossing the mighty Zambezi and returning safely, while all around me comrades were falling by the dozens.

"Then came a particularly difficult mission—we were supposed to enter deep into Rhodesia and blow up an important petrol facility. The plan was to wait in the bush for several days after the explosion before attempting to cross back. I was chosen to be the scout, and there were seven of us in all, including my brother. The raft we used was so heavy with people and explosives that it was difficult to maneuver. This was the end of the rainy season, and the current was very strong. Halfway through it became too dangerous to make noise by paddling, and we drifted well below the point that we planned to. The bank was steep and muddy, and it was hard to find a good place to hide the raft. The commanding officer decided to send one of the soldiers back to Zambia with the raft to avoid being detected. The mission was too important to be compromised, and we would have to improvise the crossing on our way back. Nobody volunteered to take the raft, and I hoped that the officer would choose my brother for the job. This mission hadn't started well, and there was something I didn't like about it. He chose someone else, and we watched him drift away and out of sight. With one fewer person to help carry, the load was very heavy, but we had to reach the target before dawn. I was trying to balance the need for speed with the need for cover. The terrain was much wetter than we expected, and I had to search for higher ground. There was also the problem of leaving as few telltale tracks as possible, although operationally that was secondary, since come daylight the main part of the mission should be over. We were approaching a main road, and the lights of an occasional car could be seen from afar. The big question came shortly after we crossed the tarmac. On the left was a small gulley that provided reasonable cover, but it was rocky, and we would make a lot of noise. The other option was to continue straight ahead on softer but more exposed ground. On a night like this sound carried farther than eyes could see, and I was tempted to go straight ahead. Something, however, didn't feel right. I tried to think like the elite Ballantyne scouts that might be waiting for us in the darkness ahead. If I were to plan an ambush, where would I do it? At first I thought, well, of course on the soft ground, since that was the route the enemy would most likely take. Then I thought that knowing that the enemy knows this, the gulley would make more sense. Crouching in darkness, I was suddenly confused about who was the enemy and who was on our side, and I couldn't make up my mind. I tried to smell the Ballantynes, but nothing came. Everybody was watching me very closely, and just before the officer gave me a nudge I thought that I felt something bad trying to reach me from the gulley and without another thought took them straight ahead.

When the shooting started I could see the lights of the bullets before I could hear them. Then they must have hit one of the rucksacks filled with dynamite, because the power of the explosion threw me into a thicket several yards away. It was such a powerful blast that they didn't even bother to check for survivors. And with the exception of Mwewe, the seagull who chose the wrong way, there were no survivors.

I must have been in a state of shock, and when I came to it was almost dawn, and it was very quiet. I saw the shattered body of my brother, and those who had been my comrades-in-arms. With only superficial wounds from the thicket that turned out to be my hiding place, I made it to the mighty Zambezi, and in full daylight I swam to safety."

During the long pause that followed Don can feel the dejection of his "comrade in drinks" and very much wants to comfort him. He wishes he could have the freedom of the lady who cleans his office and simply hug him closely to his chest. Perhaps touch his arm? No, he has hesitated too long and missed the opportunity. In the end, the only thing he can do is pour him the beer that is still left in his own bottle. This he does very slowly, drawing out the action for as long as possible, not knowing what will happen once it is finished. It is an oddly pleasant moment. He can't recall when the last time he felt like this was. Probably not since the children had grown up.

"Thank you, my friend," says Mwewe, gulping the beer down. "You wanted to know about mysteries. Well, let me tell you, the world is full of them, but the one I just told you, my friend, is among the most mysterious of them all. You see, during all the years since that night I have been unable to understand anything about it. And believe me, I have tried. Shortly after gaining independence I found the spot where I made the fatal mistake. I came on many a night and spent long hours getting to know the lay of the land, listening to the quiet rocks in the gulley, trying to understand why my bad presentiment came from the wrong direction. It had never happened to me before, and it has never happened since. The only time was when my brother was with me. Now, that is a mystery. I must have suspected that something would happen on that night, otherwise why would I hope that my brother would be chosen to take the raft back? Something was definitely odd that night. Perhaps it was because the rains had just stopped. I don't know."

This time Don is ready, and the moment Mwewe pauses he puts his hand on the other's arm. "It must have been very bad for you."

"It was bad, but it was nothing compared with what came later."

"What happened?"

"After gaining independence there was a brief period of jubilation. We returned to our homes as liberators and slowly started to build our own lives. I worked as a translator in the East German Consulate, got married, and had a son. For a while the future looked very bright. Then came the rift between ZANU and ZAPU, which was actually just another tribal conflict. It wasn't difficult for the politicians to rekindle the old hatred between the Shona and the Matabele. And so the wartime buddies became the new enemies. The situation quickly got out of control, and hundreds of innocent people were brutally killed. When I came home one day I found that my wife and my son had been murdered. Burned with the rest of the house."

Don isn't prepared for anything like this. This is too much. He is overwhelmed, and having wasted his premeditated touch earlier, he can't think of anything to do or say. He needs to urinate but can't chance leaving Mwewe just like that. The image of Claire sitting in that coffee house telling him that it was over between them forced itself into the small space in the by now overcrowded bar. He too has lost everything. He too is alone, entirely alone. No close family to speak of, no friends, and no love. Love means Claire. Yes, it still means Claire, now lost forever. *Unless...* he doesn't dare complete the thought, but he knows that it will come to haunt him later.

"Will you come with me to Matopos tomorrow?"

Don is suddenly frightened by all this excitement and needs time to think things over. Besides, he has to take care of several things, including the blood test.

"I can't come tomorrow. Perhaps later."

He is curious how Mwewe can take a day off just like that to spend with a stranger in the mountains, but quickly realizes that Mwewe must be just the type of man who can do it. A free man. So is he, as long as he stays here, provided he can keep up his courage. He tries to see the office, with Carl and Dorothy lost in attempts to comprehend what has happened to the senior partner. The picture is blurred and distant.

"I think I shall go there anyway. Several weeks have passed since my last visit, and I need the place. It helps me get in touch with myself. You see, if I could have spent some time in Matopos just before the Zambezi crossing, I would have been able to avert the disaster. No question about it, my friend."

"When you return from there, would you visit me at Sinamatella? That's where I'm staying."

"Perhaps I will," says Mwewe, and he stands up and leaves. Don feels that he has let him down. First he listens to his life story, and just when it is his turn to give something of himself, he retreats into his shell. Is he really afraid of this man of mystery? Troubled by something wild about him? Or perhaps just plain hesitant to establish friendship? Too cautious once again? Fortunately, these thoughts are cut short by his opportunity to finally use the bathroom.

That night he dreams about Iris. He isn't sure how it started, but when he wakes up in the dark room he can still see her. It was a bad dream. She was about to board the bus that would take her and the rest of the group away, and she came to say goodbye. Don can remember holding her hands and repeating again and again, "I'm sorry Iris, I don't deserve you yet…but I will try," or something like that. Then the anger was wiped from her face, and her eyes were teary. The driver of the bus was honking. She lifted her hand and brushed it gently against his unshaven face, turned slowly, and left. He wanted to shout, "Don't leave me. Oh, please don't leave me," but the words didn't come out. Then he wanted to run after her and ask her to forgive him, to stay with him, but his legs wouldn't move, and the bus left.

In the dream she was so young and beautiful, and now he feels lonely waiting for the morning to come. He wonders if he will ever see Iris again—probably not. The decision to stay was so abrupt that he never even asked for her address. Perhaps he can find her through the travel agent? No, he will never stoop to such an invasion of privacy. But what if his HIV test is positive? He will have to alert her somehow. It will be a punishment out of all proportion to his guilt. They were both consenting adults, weren't they? How can he even consider being guilty, unless he still feels bound to Claire? Is he supposed to abstain from women while she is probably indulging in promiscuous sex? Well, he suspects that that is what she is doing, but he can't really be sure about that. The suspicion is entirely based, after all, on his sense of his own inadequacy in that department. Perhaps he is wrong. Perhaps Claire is also lonely.

At this point Don has the feeling that he is being pulled toward some unfinished business from yesterday that has gotten stuck in the mud of his brain, without recalling what it is. He feels good about Claire's loneliness and wonders if they could ever make it together again. He could change for her. To get her back he is willing to change as much as it takes. In all departments. He can hear Irv warning him against looking back, and warning him against changing for someone else's sake. "The time has come for you to be yourself." And yet if she could only see him now. If he could sit with her and tell her some of his wonderful stories. So much has happened in these few short weeks. Not bad. What are a few weeks back in the big city? Nothing. Nothing ever happens. One day repeats itself again and again, and all weekends are pretty much the same as well. Don tries to recall what day it is, but he can't be sure. In Sinamatella it is easy to lose track of time, and he has to go back as far as his decision to stay in order to sort out which day it is. He is still working on it when sleep finally helps him out.

The next morning, not knowing the details of the blood test, he skips breakfast and asks Marigold to place a call for him to New York. She looks surprised, but it is only when he gets Dorothy on the answering machine that he realizes there is a six-hour time difference. It's three in the morning in New York as he listens to Dorothy saying, "You have reached the offices of Mendelson and Cartwright, Certified Public Accountants. We are sorry but we cannot take your call at this time. Please leave your name and phone number, and we will call you back as soon as possible. Thank you." He knows this recording well, and yet it sounds odd. He is tempted to leave a message, but at the sound of the tone he quickly hangs up.

With the exception of the long lines of sick people waiting to be seen, the hospital looks quite modern, and Don decides to take his chances. It takes him a while to convince the receptionist that he really wants to be tested for HIV; apparently she has never seen a "European" asking for such a service. He has to fill out several forms specifying his whereabouts and the names of his sexual partners. He realizes that for some African countries AIDS has become an epidemic of catastrophic proportions, and unless its spread is checked, their very existence is in question. A young intern in a spotless white uniform goes over his forms.

"What is your current address, sir?"

"Sinamatella."

"And where exactly is this Sinamatella?"

"In the Hwange National Park."

Don can't believe his ears that someone living in Bulawayo doesn't know about Sinamatella. Can it be because of the proximity of Matopos? One special place is all that's needed anyway. He wants to have Sinamatella as a special place of his own, and the intern's ignorance isn't entirely disappointing. He wonders whether Mwewe would know where to look for him in case he wants to.

The blood test over, he is told that the results will be available in a week. Sorry, no phones and no telegrams. His personal presence is absolutely mandatory. Don had hoped to have the answer immediately, and the idea of another long week of worry doesn't appeal to him at all. Suddenly he feels hungry, and in a small coffee shop across the street orders himself a hearty breakfast. Now that there is nothing more he can do about it he feels better, almost relieved. The sun is shining this morning, and the city has a clean and pleasant feeling to it. He enjoys a stroll along the main boulevard and admires the tall jacaranda trees. Above the entrance to a big hotel he sees AVIS printed in red and white. He rents a Toyota Corolla for one week, with unlimited mileage. It is strange driving on the left side of the road, like shaving the left cheek first, and he takes it very slowly. The roundabouts are particularly tricky and he has to figure out who has the right of way. He gets back to his hotel around noon and doesn't want to waste time waiting for Dorothy to get to the office. Instead, he sends her a cable from the post office. It is a good cable: "SELL ALL MUTUAL FUNDS, AND SEND MONEY C/O HWANGE POST OFFICE, ZIMBABWE. LETTER TO FOLLOW. DON."

Next he visits the National Parks Office, making sure that his lodge at Sinamatella will be available at least through next week. The old lady with the unusually thick lips tells him that since the tourist season is not yet in full swing it's OK, but she can't guarantee anything beyond next week. Don doesn't mind, since by then he might learn that he's infected, and who knows what he would do next anyway. This settled, he takes the Toyota on the main road to Victoria Falls and reaches the park gates just in time before they closed for the night.

Claire

Claire can't believe her ears. What is all this nonsense about Don's escapade in Africa? Why would he go to Africa of all places? Why would he go anywhere? There must be some reason. When her daughter called from Louisville she was both glad to hear from her after what must have been several months, and at the same time surprised. Naomi never calls just to establish contact; there is always a clear reason for calling her mother. For several years now Claire hasn't been comfortable with her daughter. There is always tension, as if they were competing. "Mother," she calls her, like somebody from an old British movie, never Mom, or Mama, or even Claire. It started during early adolescence, and there doesn't seem to be any relief in sight. Certainly not after she left Don. Naomi is angry with her and has told her that she will never forgive her for hurting "Daddy." "He was so helpless, and he was such a good person." Her choice of words isn't accidental; it's meant to do damage. Claire knows that Don is helpless, and she knows that he is a good person. Not once during their twenty-eight years together did he harm her intentionally. Emphasis on intentionally, because in his passive aggressive style he did harm her a lot. Ever since her therapist first used this expression she realized how right he was. Don's passive aggressive behavior is his weapon against her, and against the whole world. It has taken her years to realize that she is a victim, and a few more years to muster up the courage to put an end to it. But she never wanted to inflict pain on him. Naomi, however, doesn't believe that.

"Do you have a lover?"

"That, young lady, is no business of yours." She knows that the "young lady" gives away her anger, but can't help it. Neither can she resist the need to justify herself: "If you must know, it doesn't matter whether I have a lover or not. I left your father because I need a life of my own."

This was now more than five months ago, but the memory is still very vivid and painful. Particularly the part when Naomi complained about Claire's secrecy. "Two weeks earlier, on Thanksgiving, why did you pretend that everything was alright? To imagine that all this time you were plotting and didn't have the decency to warn me about what was about to happen." No, her young daughter doesn't mince words.

Claire, telling herself that she is the adult, has called her twice since, both calls ending in more recriminations. Realizing that she has broken up her entire family, she feels sad more than anything else. David is more understanding of her decision, but he has his own family to worry about and doesn't seem too interested in the lives of his parents. Besides, California is very far away. She has always suspected him of deliberately taking a job as far away from them as possible. *He was also suffocating and needed a life of his own,* she thought. Don suffocates himself and all the people around him. She needs fresh air. He can't give it to her even if he wants to. He can't understand the need for it. Doesn't have any concept of it.

This morning Naomi sounded very excited. "I got a letter from Dad. Did you know that he's in Africa?" No, she didn't know. When he didn't answer the phone in the evening she assumed that he had taken his standard Caribbean vacation somewhat later than usual. Under the circumstances it made sense, although she wondered how he was managing there all by himself.

"He sounds great. I'm so happy for him."

"But where in Africa is he?"

"It's somewhere in Zimbabwe. I don't know exactly where. The letter was posted in the US by a certain Mike who just came back from there. He was the tour guide. Dad wrote me that he decided to stay there for a while. Don't you think this is wonderful?"

Claire doesn't know what to think, and after some struggle she calls Dorothy. Yes, she has heard from him. Got a cable instructing her to sell all the mutual funds and send him the money. A letter that will presumably tell her more is on the way. Claire isn't worried about the money as such. Don has always been fair to her in financial matters, and even after she left he gave her full access to their joint bank account. At the same time, she feels uneasy about this cable. Does it mean that he intends to stay there indefinitely? How uncharacteristic of him. How totally uncharacteristic.

On an impulse she calls her ex-therapist and hears about a letter from a place with a strange name that Irv can't remember, dated May

23 or so. "Quite an extraordinary letter," he says, but won't say anything more. How come everybody but her knows about this? Although it doesn't make sense, she feels left out.

He then asks her how she's doing. "Oh, I'm fine, just fine," she said, but he isn't convinced.

"Do you miss him?"

"Of course I miss him, sometimes. Wouldn't anybody? I mean, after so many years, it's natural, isn't it?"

"Yes," he agreed.

Next she tells him about this fantastic evening course titled "Modern Life and Total Health" she's taking at the New School. "The instructor, Dr. Jeremy Newman, perhaps you know him, he is really great. He pulls it all together—the body and the mind, and philosophy, mostly Eastern philosophy, and post modernism…everything. I don't get how he does it. A true Renaissance man. Marion enjoys it as much as I do. You remember Marion, my best friend? We do aerobics together as well. She is a great friend, and gives me a lot of support."

Irv says that she uses the adjective "great" too often, and he hopes that she is really OK. Next he asks about her love life.

"Well," she tells him, "there was someone at the time I made the move, but it didn't work out. He was too demanding, and all I needed was some space for me. He wanted me to move in with him, and I did, but after a brief period of excitement I left. I rented this two-bedroom apartment on the Upper West Side, and it's really great. I mean, it's OK. I found a secretarial job with a small law firm so I'm also financially independent. And my diet is under control as well, so you really don't need to worry about me. You have done a good job, and I feel that I'm discovering inner sources of my own strength. But

I do worry about Don, and I hope that he knows what he's doing. I really do."

When it's over, she doesn't feel good about this conversation, and she knows that she wasn't able to fool Irv about her emotions. It surprises her that she would want to convince him that she feels OK, as if his approval is essential to her well-being. The truth is that she isn't so sure herself how she feels, and Naomi's call certainly hasn't improved matters. But even that is more complicated, since it reduces her overwhelming sense of guilt about Don. Irrespective of how much she tries to convince herself that there is no alternative, and that in the long run it's for his as much as her own good, she knows better than that. Now, on learning that this "good man"—who lived with her for twenty-eight years, who is the father of her children, and who is still her lawful husband—is acting like something is finally happening in his life, she should definitely feel less guilty. It's her decision that has made it possible. But everything is so complicated. There are so many pros and cons to everything one thinks or does that it's impossible to know how to act.

"Trust your gut feeling" was what Irv used to tell her again and again. Well, what should one do when gut feelings are all mixed up? She takes a deep breath, closes her eyes, and tries to clear her mind of thoughts, to allow her true feelings to reach the surface. Sometimes this works, but not now. *I must be trying too hard,* she tells herself. *Perhaps it will work later.* Jeremy Newman often talks about the need to free ourselves from the tyranny of thought. It keeps us limited in a shallow orbit, he says. It's obvious that he enjoys astronomy metaphors. *I wish I knew more about these things. There is so much that I would like to know, but the days are too short. If I hadn't wasted so many years on nothing, I'd be totally different now. Both physically and mentally.*

She likes her face. At fifty—not just yet, but soon—hers isn't a bad face. It has this quality that Norman, her ex-lover, referred to as fragile beauty. Sitting in front of the mirror she often tries to understand what he meant. At first she assumes that it's her eyes, but their deep darkness conveys a whole variety of expressions, some of them not at all suggestive of frailty. Then she thinks that the hint of high cheekbones is probably more relevant, but she isn't sure. Can it be the long nose, or the paleness of her skin? Her voice has a tendency to tremble just a little, particularly when she talks very softly. It's as if her lungs can't support the effort. That certainly could account for it. She likes to think of herself as a fragile beauty, and thanks Norman for bringing it to her attention. *Some words are like gifts that stay with us forever,* she thought.

She couldn't stay with Norman, though. It was all too early for her, and she was very confused at the time. If they had met once she was more settled, like now, or better yet a few months from now, it could have developed into something more serious. Norman was a very nice man, and a passionate lover. He was also trying to recover from a bad marriage, and they both needed each other. "Relationships shouldn't be based on personal needs"—another of Irv's famous statements. But aren't they all? What else could they be based on? *I certainly needed him to give me courage when I needed it most. I simply used him. Even Marion said so. She is such an honest person. I am so lucky to have her as a friend. I only wish that she would sometimes be less demanding about our diet. As long as we are in good shape there is no need to be constantly counting calories.*

Claire likes her figure, although lately she worries about her impending menopause. It's bound to start any month now, and she can't make up her mind about what do to about her hormones. Marion, who has already started taking hormones, won't even consider the alternative. But that is unfair, since she isn't at high risk for breast cancer. With all those cysts in her breasts, and her mother's history, Claire takes her gynecologist very seriously. He has urged her to consider whether it's worth the risk. Last Tuesday, an article in the science section of the *New York Times* confused her even more. It's not just hair growth that is at stake, but osteoporosis as well. Even such a simple decision as this is getting more complicated than ever.

She is an avid reader of the *Times*, and with the exception of the weekly Book Review that she reads with an almost religious tenacity, the part that interests her most is anything pertaining to health. The problem is that what seems healthy today is often found to be dangerous tomorrow. How can one know what to eat, or how much red wine to drink? How can one be sure? Lately she is much more scared about cancer, and she needs constant reassurance. For years Don tried to make her give up smoking, and she used to just shrug her shoulders as if it didn't concern her. Then, on the day she left him, she promised herself "to be good" and quit smoking. And to her great surprise, she did. It was less difficult than she had expected, despite the fact that Norman smoked occasionally. She felt virtuous, and in some compelling way it justified everything else she did. In terms of her own morale, it was the best thing that happened to her, and she often tries to visualize the progressive cleansing of her lungs. Morale is important, she knows that. Jeremy Newman can't emphasize that enough. "In modern life, our health is hostage to the swings of our daily moods. Like the moon, it is in constant change."

Suddenly everything is changing too quickly, she thought, *even Don.* What could possibly make him take a trip to Africa, and then decide to stay there? Another woman? No, that's unlikely. But then, who knows? Perhaps there is another woman. He is, after all, a decent person, and quite good looking too. Nothing special, but certainly on the good-looking side. It takes a long time to know a person intimately. *It took me many years to realize that behind the solid and peaceful exterior there was absolutely nothing. His is a reasonably charming empty shell. No gravitational force, no pull whatsoever.*

It takes her another hour of musing to admit that she is envious of Don's trip. There is something unfair about it, she feels. Whenever she suggested that they travel to some interesting place he always found hundreds of arguments against it. The cost, the distance, the climate, and the long list of dangers: bad hygiene, no decent roads, internal unrest, and the variety of strange diseases long forgotten in their part of the world. He liked to dwell on the diseases and the numerous vaccinations that they would need to have before going on the trip. She often wondered where he had gotten so much information, and whether he was thinking about it more than he admitted. She, for one, is almost obsessed with adventure travel, and enjoys lying in bed with the *Sunday Times* travel section. Her old atlas is too heavy to put on top of the blanket, and she keeps it on the floor. Several times she would pick it up and search for places with exotic names, provided they have nothing to do with the Caribbean.

Marion and Claire have decided to travel abroad at least once a year, and they are forever planning. Claire enjoys planning almost as much as her friend does, but so far nothing seems to be settled. For a while they thought of going to China, but a young nephew of Marion's had just returned from China and strongly advised against it. "The place is too chaotic," he said. "Dirty and chaotic." Next they discarded India for very much the same reason, although after listening to Jeremy Newman they had second thoughts. Kenya was becoming outrageously expensive, and it now appears that they might take a European vacation sometime in August. Although she is looking forward to visiting Paris, and perhaps Italy, Europe isn't going anywhere, and there are so many more exciting places to see. Like Zimbabwe, for instance. She knows about Zimbabwe from a brochure devoted entirely to the Victoria Falls and the Zambezi River. She ordered it from a California travel agency called Wild Safaris that specializes in arranging highly esoteric guided tours: Sahara crossing by night, following the Silk Route in central Asia, Antarctica exploration, rafting the Orinoco in Venezuela, retracing Stanley's search for Livingstone, Victoria Falls and the mighty Zambezi. What is Europe compared to these? Something mild and predictable; something that Don might do. It is confusing to think that while he of all people is somewhere in Zimbabwe, she will be dutifully following the prescribed tourist routes of Paris.

It is time for her to head to the gym, and she is glad to leave the apartment and venture out to negotiate Broadway during one of its busiest hours. Slightly confused by what is happening, but steadfast in her determination to live a full and meaningful life, she walks briskly to her workout. Once there she will try to improve her record on the treadmill. It's good for her, and it makes her a better person.

Fear

The road leading from Sinamatella down into the bush is already familiar. Since getting the car, Don has taken it out twice a day—an early morning drive just before sunrise, and a late afternoon drive through the sunset. He has witnessed the beauty of the sunsets before, but the sunrises are relatively new. *If you live in a big city working nine to five, you never see the sun rise above the horizon,* he thought. *How many sunrises have I seen in my life? How many have I missed?* He recalls reading somewhere about Hemingway promising himself to never miss a sunrise. What a wonderful promise, particularly for someone waking up with a hangover from drinking late into the night. He doesn't know much about Hemingway's private life and thinks that he should find out more.

As he leaves the main road and enters one of the river circuits the light is just starting to turn golden. He knows that the gold will peak in another hour and a half, and then it will be downhill again. The darkness in these parts falls very quickly, and he will have to be sure not to miss the closing time of the main gate. It is easy to lose sense of time, particularly if you observe some interesting animals. The previous evening he almost didn't make it because of the huge hyena crossing the road. It was already twilight, and he couldn't believe his eyes it was so large. "Lucky" had said that the females are much taller than the males, so this must have been a female. She was carrying something in her mouth that looked like a piece of cloth but turned out to be the skin of an antelope.

Don wants to make sure that on his way back the sun is behind him, and he plans the entire drive very carefully. It will bring him to a remote waterhole that he has never visited before, and which Ian the barman mentioned as a particular favorite drinking spot for elephants. Don likes elephants, and watching them drink and bath is especially enjoyable. There is something captivating about the way a herd approaches water and after quenching its thirst starts to play around. The very young and adolescent animals are particularly flamboyant, and their jolly trumpeting carries over long distance.

Waiting for the results of his HIV test is very difficult for him, and most of the long week is still ahead of him. During his bush drives he doesn't think much about his problem, and they are by far the best part of his day. By now he has gotten used to driving on the left side of the road, although it doesn't make much of a difference on the remote roads inside the park. Once far enough from the gate he rarely encounters another car and stays in the center of the dusty road. On most occasions the approach of another vehicle is clearly signaled by a thick cloud of dust, leaving plenty of time to close the windows and move to the left. His little Toyota produces a cloud of its own, and he likes to watch it in the rearview mirror. Yesterday morning the wind was coming from behind too fast and the red dust caught him unprepared, covering everything inside the car. It had a distinct smell, and licking his lips he tasted its mild bitterness.

On his left he sees a silver backed jackal trotting casually along. Behind him in a clearing in the bush are several zebra and wildebeest mixed together. He slows down to get a better view, and one of the zebras becomes alert, sniffing for the nature of the intruder. He stops and aims the binoculars that are hanging from his neck at the herd that now appears to be larger than he originally thought. Several wildebeest start to run and then stop just as suddenly. Their movements are exaggerated, as if they need to give vent to enormous pent-up energy. Even the jackal now takes brief notice of the car before resuming his easy trot. The disturbance caused by his entry into the scene gives Don an odd sense of importance. It is quite pleasant to be noticed and viewed as potentially dangerous. The contrast to the way he would be totally ignored on entering into a metropolitan scene couldn't have been greater. He knows that some people can't be ignored even on a busy New York street, but he just isn't one of them. Iris can't be ignored anywhere. He tries to conjure up her image—the smooth blond hair, the well-defined features of her face, and her perfect figure. He left her figure for the end, savoring the memory of his brief access to that young and exquisite body. From there it is only a short distance to remembering HIV and he has to resume driving to escape his mounting anxiety.

The road is now entering a narrow ravine with steep banks on both sides. Here the bush is quite dense, and Don hopes that with some luck he might catch a glimpse of a greater kudu. He had seen two males on one of the morning walks at Robins Camp and was fascinated by their stately heads, adorned by long and perfectly symmetrical curved horns. Kudu males are notorious for their shyness, and despite looking for them, he hasn't seen another one since. They prefer the safety of the dense acacia bush, and with the exception of an encounter near an open drinking place, unless one is very lucky, the chances of seeing them are rather slim. He is driving very slowly, carefully watching both sides of the road.

Suddenly, right in front of him, he sees a large herd of elephants. They are in the middle of the narrow road, not more than fifty yards ahead. Don shifts to neutral and lets the car glide gently a little closer. When he is twenty yards from the herd he brakes and switches off the engine. This is exactly what Ian told him to do, explaining that elephants hate noise, and hate the smell of petrol. "They are gentle creatures, but are easily provoked. Make sure to respect their right of way, and don't do anything rash," he had said. Making a sudden noise or a sudden movement could be particularly dangerous. Don tries to use the binoculars, but the huge beasts loom so large that the magnification is useless. The herd consists of several adult females, and a mixture of adolescents and small calves. There must be at least twenty-five of them, and they are crowding the narrow road ahead. They don't seem to be moving and are just milling around. The water hole is still several miles ahead, and Don has no idea what has brought them to this spot. One of the adults—*perhaps the matriarch,* thought Don—sees the car and apparently doesn't approve at all, because she lifts her trunk, fans out her ears, and starts walking toward him. He looks in the rearview mirror before starting the engine to back up, and can't believe his eyes. The mirror is filled with elephants approaching him from behind. He quickly turns his head and sees more elephants coming down the steep bank on the left. They are very quiet, and were it not for the occasional breaking of a branch, no sound would have given them away.

Oh my God. Oh my G-o-d. *Why bother about a three letter word now? What am I going to do? What are they going to do? Trapped.* Tra-p-ped. *It must have been a trap, with all these elephants hiding behind the bush while the others acted as a decoy,* Don thought. The big female stops a few yards in front of the car, and Don can now see her calf walking slowly behind her. *This must be very dangerous—I should tell Ian about this at the bar, provided I get out of here alive. These elephants are huge, not like the ones in Irv's pictures, or the ones in the political cartoons in the* New York Times. *I wish these were donkeys instead.*

He is now completely surrounded, and there is no way to escape. He holds tightly to the engine key but doesn't dare switch it on. His grip on it is so strong that his fingers start to cramp. His heart is racing, and he can feel its wild beating in his throat and in his temples. Any time now one of these huge beasts will turn over the little Toyota and trample on it in great fury. He knows about the plight of the African elephants from poachers, and their hate of humans. Elephants never forget. If even a single one of them has had some bad experience with a human, now is its chance to retaliate. He can see the headlines in the papers: "Elephants Kill American Tourist." Small headlines. Nobody cares anyway. Claire widowed by the rage of an endangered species. "Cornered Elephants Strike Back." *Wait a minute, who is the one cornered here? And why me? I have never hurt an elephant, or any other creature for that matter. Even the cockroaches in New York must realize that. Unfair, the whole thing is extremely unfair. Yes, extremely unfair, all this happening just when I could have started living.*

His growing anger gives him enough courage to fully turn his head, and he sees that a huge bull elephant is approaching him with great strides. There is not enough room on the tiny road for him to pass the car, and the banks here are particularly steep. *This is it,* thought Don. *This is it. What am I supposed to do now? Review my life in three seconds?* The bull is so tall that for a moment Don thinks that he will simply step over the car, there is enough room under his huge belly. Then, even as he is watching with fascination the long and strangely curved penis of the creature approaching him, he has enough time to realize that three seconds is more than he needs to sum up his life. Even just one second would do. Nothing. Nada. Nothing comes of nothing. Nothing ever has. What a waste.

The bull has now reached the car and starts to pass it on the right. Realizing that the space is too narrow, he leans to the extreme right, and like a ballerina doing a pirouette, manages to squeeze his huge bulk through without even touching the Toyota. Not even the slightest touch. While he is moving past Don's window, he can see his long eyelashes. Don thinks that they are very beautiful. The eye has a sad expression, and the eyelashes are exquisite. As the elephant passes to join the herd ahead, Don wants to cry. He loves this elephant. He loves all *el-ep-h-an-ts*. The midpoint is unpronounceable. He tries to voice the *h* several times, one after another, but it doesn't sound right. *Perhaps the center is not so important anyway,* Don thought, *since this bull was able to shift his weight all the way to the right just so that he could pass me in peace.* Yes, he loves him. He loves the entire world, even himself.

It takes almost two hours before he can extricate himself from the herd. The different families greet each other by touching their trunks and the young bulls wrestle among themselves. On two subsequent occasions Don became very tense again, but never as tense as when his elephant managed to pass him. The first time was when the calf of the angry female up ahead discovered the little Toyota and started running to explore it. Perhaps she thought it was another calf. Her mother rushed after her, barely stopping her in the nick of time. After chastising her youngster, she turned toward the car itself, and lifting her trunk all the way, made a sudden squeaking sound that gave Don goose bumps. Standing poised for an attack, she looked ominous, but after a while she relaxed.

The second time was when his elephant and another big bull started to shove each other in a display of strength. Don watched with obvious partiality. This went on for some time, and then the other elephant started to back up toward the car. Both contestants were totally absorbed in their mock fight and couldn't see the tiny car that blocked their way. Should he honk? Start the engine and attempt to reverse toward all the elephants standing behind him? In the end the only thing that Don could think to do was wish they would stop. Everything suddenly depended on whether his wish would work, and whether it would work in time. Then they stopped, and Don thought of Mwewe and his mysteries.

Finally, just as the sun is setting, the herd starts to split up into smaller family units, and each in its turn slowly climbs the bank of the ravine. By now there is very little fear left, and he feels exhausted. He is struck by the recognition that during the entire episode he never once noticed the golden color coming and going. Nor did he notice the time. The smell of the huge herd and the steaming heaps of fresh dung scattered all over the road is very powerful, and he hopes that somehow he will always be able to recall it in the future. It would be terrible to lose it. He inhales deeply several times before making his way back to Sinamatella.

As it turns out, there are more surprises in store for him before the day is over, for on the tiny table on his poorly lighted porch there is a letter addressed to Mr. Don Mendelson, Sinamatella, Hwange National Park, Zimbabwe. The familiar stamps are all over the envelope, and it has come by express mail from the United States. There is no return address, and while clumsily tearing it open with his shaking hands, anything seems possible. In his hurry to resolve the mystery he jumps straight to the end of the letter. The bold and somewhat uneven handwritten note ends with "Love, Iris." Now he knows, and he feels a complex mixture of disappointment and excitement at the same time. As he starts reading he feels cheated by knowing the end. A letter like this should be read without knowing the end.

Dear Don,

He approves of the formal, old-fashioned greeting with the correct punctuation, but where is the date? He is distressed that the letter is undated, and there isn't enough light to look closely at the stamps for that. The letter continues:

I don't know if this letter will ever reach you, as by now, you may have left the place where we last met. It's a beautiful place, and I hope it will do for you what you expect it to. My need to write this letter is perhaps greater than the need to send it, although I do hope that it will find you.

The brief time that we spent together has been much more meaningful to me than you might think. Yes, I know that it all started as a highly charged sexual encounter, but after having the opportunity to get to know you better, it became much more than that. I learned to care about you deeply, and I still do. That was why I was offended when you kept your thoughts from me about leaving the group and staying in Africa. I felt that I was cheated of our continued intimacy. Realizing that my own feelings were obviously unrequited really hurt.

Don makes a mental note to come back to this word later.

It especially saddened me because I knew that there were so many things that I wished to share with you, and the opportunity was suddenly gone.

You are such a wonderful, caring man and your honest and unassuming modesty is more precious than all the false macho achievements so presumptuously cultivated by most of the men I come across.

What a sentence. So young and yet so mature.

I am well aware of your need for solitude, and respect it. I also hope that it will help you overcome your hurt. If and when you have reached the point that you feel you are ready for companionship, please remember me. I have learned that good people are hard to come by, and I don't want to lose you.

When you return to the United States you can reach me at the number written below. And if you decide to stay, a single word from you would bring me flying back across half the globe to you.

Love,

Iris

His first reaction is one of total disbelief, and he has to read the letter several times before he can move to other things. What could this beautiful and intelligent modern woman possibly find in him that was appealing? Perhaps his awkwardness? Don remembers reading in some magazine article about the strong impact that helpless men sometime have on women. *Must be the mothering instinct. Well, I certainly provided her with more than enough of a challenge in that department. On top of that, the impotence might have helped too,* Don thought. His subsequent performance was her personal triumph. Now he misses her, and he wishes that he wouldn't worry so much about HIV. It is degrading to think about this loving woman as the source of a deadly virus, and it is unfair. Even objectively it doesn't make much sense. Iris isn't someone he just picked up off the street. Nor is she a drug user, as far as he can tell. It is her sexual experience that bothers him. He believes that it must be based on having a great number of "highly charged sexual encounters" with many partners. Unless she had a particularly good teacher. Although that would make it safer, Don feels jealous thinking about her that way.

While walking to the bar he tries to imagine what it would be like if she stayed with him at Sinamatella. Joined him on the bush drives. Saw the elephants. Spent the long evenings in silence watching the stars. And later, in bed, waking up his long-dormant craving, slowly guiding him in both receiving and giving pleasure. He feels dizzy imagining her soft and full body clinging to his through the night, every night. Oh, how he wants that. How good it is wanting her. Walking under the starry night, gently touching the letter in his left breast pocket, he feels vigorous and very much alive.

The bar is almost completely filled with people; there must be a new group of tourists that arrived this afternoon. He sits next to Ian's counter, pours himself a cold Castle, and waits for his chance to tell him about the elephants. It isn't something he is willing to do in a short period of time while Ian is serving other customers. The story has to be told without interruptions, or it will lose its magic. Mwewe had told his story with the audience fully committed. He wonders about Mwewe, and whether he will ever see him again. Then, halfway into his beer, he lifts his head and for the first time looks at the company sharing this space.

They are an eclectic bunch and were probably organized as a group only in Harare. At the table closest to him three young men, obviously Italians, are loudly talking about mountain climbing, because words like Kilimanjaro, Mount Kenya, and Ruwenzori often punctuate the pleasant melody. They all have a high-elevation tan of the kind he has seen among his friends who love to ski. He wonders whether they are planning to do rock climbing in the Matopos. Next to them is an elderly couple speaking English with a distinct South African accent. He can't hear anything they're saying, but he likes the softness of the vowels. Behind them, close to the wall, a family of four Americans is in the process of adding another table and a few chairs to make room for their friends who have just come in. The father is very tall and heavy, while his wife is exactly the opposite. They are all drinking Castle beers, including their two adolescent daughters who can't be more than fourteen and fifteen years old. Privileges of the bush. The newcomers are a woman of fifty and a young man half her age. Mother and son? Lovers? A married couple? She is blond and is wearing lots of makeup. Probably lovers. Don is struck by the intensity of his own stereotypes. Next he will be sure that she is outrageously rich, and the young man is after her money. He likes the way she waits for him to help her into her chair, like at a stylish restaurant. The young Italians must have been observing this too, because all of a sudden they stop talking. Ian gives him a wink and proceeds to wipe a glass with unnecessary vigor. The two girls move closer to each other looking for the opportunity to exchange meaningful glances. Only the South African couple is obviously unaffected by any of this, caressing their wine glasses and conversing quietly.

Don is struck by the notion that the bar is filled with such varied humanity. He wonders how many good stories could be told by all of them combined. Well, tonight at least, with the exception of what Ian could come up with, his story would probably rank among the best. He thinks about how quickly he made the transition from a leisurely game drive to a life-threatening ordeal. One moment you are OK, and the next you are a goner. Almost like when Claire told him that morning that she was leaving. Is life so precarious? Are we all lulled into an illusion of safety while underneath the thin protective layer danger constantly looms? Like a cancerous cell stubbornly dividing? Or a deadly virus stealthily invading a healthy body? Three more days until his trip to the hospital in Bulawayo. Three long days and nights before his judgment.

Don is famished and wonders when the others will leave for the restaurant and leave him alone with Ian and his story. The Italians have just ordered another round of beers, and that means at least another thirty minutes. Then an idea strikes him with such force that he can barely remain seated. Why tell the story today? How often can he expect to find a story like this? Why not keep it just for himself for a while longer? Why not tell it tomorrow? Or even never tell it at all? He quickly gulps down the beer in his glass, waves his goodbye to Ian, and without casting a single glance at the rest of the group, his left hand fondling his breast pocket, he goes to order himself a steak.

The next morning, shortly after breakfast, he drives to the town of Hwange to see whether his money has arrived. Hwange is a sleepy godforsaken place, with only one redeeming feature, the huge baobab tree on the hill that dominates the entire surrounding area. It is so big that he can see its rough silhouette from a great distance on his way to the post office below. The money is there, but he has to fill out several forms that are checked and rechecked by different clerks who have to pass his passport back and forth as if the post office has never seen a money transfer before. While he waits for this to be cleared up, he thinks about how he has no idea about the stock exchange, and whether he has lost a lot of money by selling the mutual funds. He realizes that he couldn't care less, and he doesn't even bother to calculate the amount of money due to him given the current exchange rate. When he insisted that Dorothy be given signature privileges he had thought of it as purely a matter of convenience. Now it turns out to have been very convenient indeed. Since he didn't bring his checkbook with him to Africa there is a limit to how much he can spend using his MasterCard. He is probably well above his limit, and he knows what is in store for him. After the grace period the bank will send a gentle reminder followed by a rather harsh notice, suspension of privileges, and ultimately a threat to his credit score. It makes him laugh to think that for his entire professional life he has built impeccable credit only to throw it away in a moment of bravado. Very much like unprotected sex. Yes, he needs the cash, especially since he has no idea how long he might stay.

He takes half of the money in Zimbabwe dollars, and his pockets are bulging so much that he can hardly sit in the car. It is a good feeling that gives him a sense of freedom. The winding road takes him up toward the Baobab Hotel, and the tree itself. It is a hot day and sitting in the easy chair positioned on the manicured grass in the shadow of the gigantic, ancient tree, he orders a glass of cold beer. Indulgence is something that has never occurred to him before, but he can appreciate the temptation involved. The tree is magnificent, and so is the view, although nothing compared with Sinamatella itself. From the moment he saw his very first Baobab, Don has been impressed by its power. The thick trunk is like a limitless reservoir of energy, from which the relatively tiny branches sprout in an incongruous manner. Mike had told them that the Bushmen believe that baobabs are planted by a hyena roots up, out of spite. They remind him of a picture from biology class of a brain cell sending out branches in all directions. Life as movement from the inside out, establishing new connections.

Suddenly, without knowing why, Don is gripped by anxiety, as if the cells in his brain have established contact with some dangerous thought. Sensing that it may have something to do with the tree, he leaves in hurry, driving back to the park. It has been some time since he felt this anxious, and the game reserve is good for him. Certain types of problems can't occur during his stay in Sinamatella; in fact, they are absolutely impossible during his time in Sinamatella. Absolutely Impossible During Sinamatella. Absolutely Impossible During Sinamatella. *A-I-D-S*. While obviously shaken by the message that has come from within, he can't be sure whether it is good or bad. Does it mean that what he considers impossible has turned into AIDS, or alternatively, that AIDS is something that is absolutely impossible? Fortunately, the need to concentrate on driving helps, and by the time he reaches Sinamatella he feels much better.

Mwewe arrives shortly after lunch. Although Don's lodge is quite far from the parking lot, from where he is sitting he recognizes him the moment he gets off the tourist bus. There is no surprise, as if he has expected him to come at any moment. Mwewe has a powerful handshake and is obviously glad to see Don again. "I see that you are still here. That's good." His voice has a distinct tremor and sounds very excited. The trip to Matopos turns out to have been more important than he could have possibly anticipated, and he is sorry that Don didn't come with him. "You could hear the silence. It really spoke this time." Don wonders whether he too would have heard the silence. Perhaps one needs special ears for that? He thinks about telling him that he has also heard some amazing things lately, but all he can say is one of Irv's standard phrases: "Tell me. Tell me all about it."

They bring out another armchair from the room, and from where they are sitting on the porch they can see a good deal of the park below. The animals are all hiding from the heat, and not a single one can be seen on the plains or near the river. "It's hard to believe that so much life is down there where nobody can see it," says Don. For a moment he isn't sure whether he should say "life" or "wildlife." He isn't sure whether it makes much of a difference.

"Yes, life has the capacity to hide for long periods of time," says Mwewe. Why does everything he says sound like something taken out of a philosophy book? Or a sermon? Does he ever engage in small talk? How about the weather? No, the weather figures in his touch with his special gifts. Food? Clothing? These might qualify for small talk if only they were easily available. Not in Africa. He wonders what might be regarded as small talk here.

Mwewe tells him about Matopos. He talks about the color of the huge rocks, and about the wind. The wind played different tunes at different locations. And the caves. Those that are relatively easily accessible and those that are not. The caves where ancestral spirits live, and some of them are off limits, too dangerous to enter. He tells him about his struggle with the temptation to enter such a cave, and how only nightfall released him from its grip. Don sees himself as an adolescent struggling for hours with the temptation to masturbate, until somebody knocked on his door and released him from the temptation. Once on a Caribbean vacation they stood near a cliff overhanging the ocean. Sixty feet below, where the surf pounded the rocks, there was a small green pool. Naomi was six at the time, and he wondered what would happen were she to fall into the deep pool. Would he jump after her to try and save her? Would he? The idea kept pestering him and testing him throughout that entire vacation. The night was very cold, Mwewe tells him, and he built himself a small fire. The wind made the shadows dance across the rocks. The dance started as a slow one, but gained speed, like during the Bushmen healing trance. In the morning he felt healed of bad thoughts, as if they had been washed away from his soul. And he felt that his gifts were his again to be used. It was a great responsibility, and he was afraid of it.

On his way here, as his bus stopped in a small village, he saw an old man walking in the distance, and then it occurred to him that he would fall soon. Things like that sometimes happened and he couldn't control them. Now he is afraid that on his way back he will learn that the old man has died. He remembers how since childhood he has always been scared of images that foretell the future. He knows that his spiritual gifts must not be abused, and that he should use them with great care. The problem is that sometimes they are forced on him. Like this vision of the old man falling, or when he saw him, Don.

"What was it you saw?"

"It doesn't matter, it was nothing important."

"You must tell me what it was!"

"Nothing important, I told you already."

Don is frightened, almost as frightened as yesterday during his encounter with the elephants. He doesn't believe that it is unimportant. Mwewe must have come all this distance just to warn him.

"Mwewe," he says, emphasizing his first opportunity to use his name, "you can tell me what it was. I can take it, and I need to know."

"Alright. I saw you embarking on a long journey, from which there was no way back."

"Does it...does it mean death?" He is surprised how easy it is to say the word.

"I don't know. I don't think so. It could be any number of things. Like this trip to Africa, for instance."

"How did you see it? And how could you know that there was no way back?"

"You never looked back. You tried, but just couldn't."

"Was I naked?"

"No, you were not naked."

Don finds some encouragement in the fact that in Mwewe's vision he was not naked, and he thinks it best not to pursue this any further.

"Thank you for telling me," he says, and a few seconds later he adds, "and now let me tell you about yesterday." He then totally immerses himself in his story, as if it's the only way to push the bad omen out of his consciousness.

"My story is about elephants," he begins, although he isn't so sure that it is about elephants. Of course elephants play an important role in it, but the essence of the story seems to be something else. "It is about elephants, and about fear, and about coincidence. It is also about other things that I cannot yet understand. As a man of mystery, you should find it interesting. Let me start with the coincidence. What are the chances that close to a hundred elephants from eight or ten different families will come together at one particular spot at the same time? Very small. Now add to it the chances that this spot is in a ravine with steep banks that make the elephants' movement extremely difficult. Very small indeed. In addition, the meeting has to take place at the exact moment when an insignificant car enters the ravine, so as to block its line of retreat. And that car, mind you, must have a single occupant, a certified public accountant from New York."

Don likes the way he has begun his story, and Mwewe likes it too. He pulls his chair just a bit closer, and instead of comfortably reclining, he moves his body forward into an awkward and tense position.

"Were there bulls?"

"Yes, several of them."

"And how about little calves? Any calves?"

"Lots of calves."

"You were lucky to come out of there alive."

Don is ecstatic, as if he has somehow earned his survival by his luck. Mwewe knows the bush, and if he says so, it must have been a case of extreme luck, or else he would have started his long journey of no return right there and then. Once the idea hits him he can't resist asking when exactly it was that Mwewe saw him embarking on his journey. But it turns out to be a dead end, and somewhat reluctantly he returns to his story. His mind keeps wandering, and the rest of the story doesn't match the quality of the beginning. Not even when he talks about the eyelashes. He thinks that it might have something to do with the fact that while talking he doesn't actually see the elephants. It is all language and no imagery. And yet, just a moment ago he could summon the image without any problems. Talking, though, makes it tricky; one has to go on finishing sentences whether one's internal movie follows in tandem or not.

When Don finishes telling the story, Mwewe asks him how he felt when the big bull was coming at him from behind, and Don says that for a moment—and it had felt like a long moment because time seemed to slow down—everything depended on the bull's choice about a single movement. Mwewe nods, suggesting that Don can now better understand the way he felt when scouting enemy ground across the Zambezi. Only that feeling is more complex, combining as it does Don's apprehension with the elephant's choice of the route. However, that is only a technical difference, since Mwewe is sure that by now Don could see things from the elephant's point of view. Maybe that's why he wasn't so scared in the first place. Don argues that he was scared, very scared, but when Mwewe asks him whether he lost control of his bladder it is obvious that there was fear and there was *fear*.

At first he feels belittled by this last question, since it suggests that he is making too much fuss over a benign game drive. Mwewe, however, thinks otherwise, and impressed on him how smart he had been not to try anything stupid like honking the horn or starting the engine. "You kept your cool," he says. "Very few people would have been able to do that."

At this point Don, having deliberately skipped the part about wishing the two wrestling elephants away, mentions it for the first time, emphasizing that the oddest thing was that it worked. At the very last moment. "I see that you are on your way to become a man of mystery yourself," says Mwewe without even the slightest hint of cynicism. "A few more weeks in this place, and who knows what may happen."

Don agreed.

✶✶✶✶✶

That evening he has Ian all to himself. The bus with the assorted tourists had left just before sunset and Mwewe caught a ride with them. They will spend the night at Gwaai River and proceed to Bulawayo the following morning. Don tries to convince Mwewe to stay longer, perhaps even two full days so that they can take the long trip together, but he won't even consider it.

"You came all this distance just for an hour or two of conversation?"

"Yes, why not? The time was short, but well spent. Now I must go."

Mwewe then gave him his business card, in case their roads crossed again. Jordan (Mwewe) Mpulia, M.Sc. Geologist, Ganzell Mining Company, Total House, Bulawayo. Don writes his personal information on the back of a yellow receipt from the Hwange petrol station. "Watch yourself," says Mwewe as he boards the bus, leaving behind a mixture of premonition and warmth.

With all this cash Don feels rich and invites Ian for an Amstel instead of the traditional Castle. While he is warming up for the story he wants to share with him, he mentions Mwewe's visit to Matopos. "You and my African friend have something in common, since both of you seem to be entirely in awe of that place."

Ian asks about Mwewe and Don tells him that they met in a bar and that he is a trained geologist, and a good story teller. Nothing about mysteries. That is a private affair. Then, as they are into their second Amstel (Don can't taste the difference but pretends otherwise), he mentions that yesterday he followed Ian's suggestion and drove to the waterhole.

"How was it? Did you see elephants?"

"I never reached the place, but yes, I saw a lot of elephants. In fact, my story is about elephants, and about fear, and about coincidence. It is also about other things that I cannot yet understand."

Even as he is unfolding his tale he realizes that this is cheating. Instead of describing what was certainly a very meaningful event, and even though he wasn't so terrified as to lose control of his bladder, it was a very frightening event just the same, and he was simply repeating the way he had told it before. *Something is very wrong here,* he thought, but he is by now too committed and can't stop it. He promises himself that he'll seriously look into it later, when he's alone. Lately too much has happened too quickly, and he hasn't had enough time to himself to work things out. He recalls how happy he was last night when he decided not to tell his story. Now it has come out of him ringing false. Like the over-rehearsed performance of the professional tourist guide. *In front of you, ladies and gentlemen, you'll see elephants. Please pay attention to the calves under the bellies of their mothers. Now you may wish to look in your rearview mirror and observe more elephants that were not there a moment ago. You are witnessing an instance of being completely surrounded.*

With some difficulty, taking advantage of longer-than-usual pauses, he manages to both talk and think about it at the same time. However, when Ian says that he is fortunate to have seen this rather than fortunate to have come out alive, Don's interest is rekindled. It is very rare to actually witness "the meeting of the clans," as Ian calls it, not to mention actually sit in the midst of it.

"What do you mean by this 'meeting of the clans'?"

"That is exactly what it was. Once in a while all the elephants in a large region of the park organize a meeting of all the families. It must be an awesome sight."

"But how do they pull of off? I mean, how do they coordinate such a thing?"

"They communicate over long distances using very low frequency sounds that are below our range of hearing. This was discovered quite recently. I actually saw a film where they have recorded those sounds and played them back to unsuspecting elephants, and they all converged on the loudspeaker."

Don is desperately trying to understand the implications all this might have on his story. But there is an important part missing.

"And what is the purpose of these meetings?"

"Nobody has managed to figure this one out yet. Some biologists think that it's an opportunity for them to exchange information about the conditions in the park. Like a convention. I've even heard someone suggest that it serves as a census to get an estimate of the population pressure on their resources."

"What could they possibly do with such information?"

"Oh, you would be surprised what elephants can do. For instance, if there are too many of them, the females may skip an estrus cycle."

"You seem to know a lot about elephants."

"Not so, considering how much there is to know. But I do like them…very much."

There seems to be little they can say to each other after this, and Don takes the first opportunity to excuse himself and retire for some privacy. He knows that there is a long evening ahead, and that he should make good use of it.

Sinamatella, June 3

Dear Irv,

It has been a few days since I last wrote to you, and so much has taken place that I hardly know where to begin. As you can see, I write less often when things are happening; I mean actual things, not just thoughts. Right now, however, my main purpose is to clarify my own thinking on a variety of issues that seem to have piled up recently. In fact, "my need to write this letter is perhaps greater than the need to send it." This is a direct quote from Iris whose letter arrived here yesterday. You still haven't heard about my relationship with Iris; somehow I keep postponing writing about it. Perhaps it is just as well. What you ought to know, however, is that I slept with her on two consecutive nights, although the first doesn't count. Shortly after that, I decided to stay here, she left, and I started to worry about having contracted AIDS. At first I told myself that this was "Absolutely Impossible During Sinamatella" (this is my own phrase that I may elaborate on later), but my obsessive-compulsive disposition quickly got the upper hand. So I got myself to a hospital for an HIV test and should be able to get the results in two days. I can anticipate some of your interpretations about why I invented this new worry, but that doesn't help much. The truth is that until I hear that I am clean, nothing can possibly comfort me. Yes, your patient is suddenly obstinately clinging to life. I suppose one might consider this part of it to be a good sign.

While in town for the test I met a man with some strange gifts. He is a geologist by training, but a great part of his work is accomplished by the less conventional means of clairvoyance. However, his special gifts failed him when he needed them most, and he holds himself responsible for the death of his brother and several other comrades-in-arms. His wife and son were burned alive in the disturbances following independence. He has an odd mixture of rationality and appreciation of its limits. I am confident that you too would have liked him. An ancient spirit in modern clothes, he calls himself "a man of mystery." Today he came all the way to Sinamatella to warn me that in his mind he saw me embarking on a long journey from which there was no way back. He meant well and had no way of knowing that my brain is the worst type of brain to be told something like that.

At this point Don has to stop. He has had a long day and feels tired. Also, he doesn't know how to go on, at least not right away. Writing, he has found, is a good way to organize one's thoughts, but only those at the periphery of a major commotion. Moving closer to its center requires more than that. This morning in Hwange he forgot to buy a stronger electric bulb. The one he has can't be more than forty watts, and even that is in doubt. Perhaps it would be enough if the light were more focused, but the lamp has no shade on it and the light shines in all directions, diluted by the size of the room. The ceiling is so high that even his smallest movement produces huge shadows that dance all over the place. He thinks of Mwewe sitting by his fire near the forbidden cave watching the shadows dancing on the surrounding rocks. *Was it there, perhaps, that he saw this journey of no return?* Don is too spent to start seriously worrying again. Worrying, he has realized, takes a lot of effort. Fatigue helps; he should write this to Irv.

He must have fallen asleep in his armchair, because his left arm is numb. The image in his head starts to recede, and he tries desperately to hold onto it. Something about it makes so much sense that he isn't sure whether it has come to him as a dream or during the twilight state between sleep and wakefulness. The image is set in a gigantic hourglass that reminds him of some kind of coffee maker, only instead of containing sand it was filled with light. The walls are covered and dark, and the light seems to converge on the small opening dividing the two chambers. He realizes that in order to see it this way he must be inside the hourglass. As the light moves from the wider section toward the narrow one, it becomes brighter and more concentrated, hurting his eyes. Then, as the light passes through the bottleneck, it starts to expand once more. The hourglass must be lying on its side, because there is no need to flip it upside down to start the process over again. He feels like he is swimming back and forth on the current of light. Zeroing in on the narrow opening he sees the words "AIDS" very clearly but very small, as if he is looking through the wrong end of his binoculars. Squeezing through the passage the word is pushed by the current ahead of him and then it starts expanding, each letter moving in a different direction. He tries to follow the letters that now look to him like words, but soon loses them in the distance. Then, going the other way, the letters appear again in his peripheral vision and coalesce just before he passes back to the other side. Even as he is making the transition into full consciousness he knows that somewhere there is also a baobab tree with its roots in the air, but he can't see where or how. The only thing he can retain is the idea of it.

The silence is now absolute, and he tries to listen to it, but without much success. His watch indicates that it is well past midnight, and he realizes that tomorrow he will get the results of his HIV test. Then, just as he is wondering whether he should go to bed or try to write some more, he sees the word "HIV" clearly in his mind exactly the way he would set up his words before cutting them to pieces. However, instead of looking for the midpoint he lets it drift off into the distance where it visibly disintegrates before his eyes, each letter going its own way, sprouting new words. *Hoping In Vain,* he reads, clearly recognizing the original source of each word.

What a discovery! He runs it once more, only this time the letters turn into *High In Value,* followed by *High In Vanity,* and *Hoping Is Valuable.* It is obvious that there are many different solutions to this kind of problem, and with some effort, he can guide the process in almost any direction he wishes. It is like navigating the hourglass with marvelous expertise. He lets go of HIV and tries his hand at the word "positive." To his surprise the solution comes immediately: *Punishment Of Stupidly Irresponsible Transient Impulsive Vain Experience.* This isn't exactly proper English, but it makes a lot of sense just the same. Don enjoys the feeling that it is all coming from within. He sees himself in the form of a brain cell reaching out to sprout new connections. *Wait a minute,* he thought, *each new word can be seen as yet another starting point to produce new meanings. Like the branches of a tree.* Words, all words, are raw material. "Language is to the mind more than light is to the eye." Who had said that? He must have read it in that calendar of his before throwing it away.

Fully awake now, and obviously excited, he returns to the letter. After reading the last part, he decides to let go of Mwewe. He is not ready for him yet.

June 4, after midnight

Recently I have made two observations that have some relevance to your profession. Actually, they could be seen as two different angles of a single observation. I have found that we have a deep need to keep some information to ourselves. Don't be mistaken, Irv, I am not referring to anything that has to do with painful memories or thoughts. On the contrary, what I have in mind is something that is quite pleasant and would probably never be repressed. Here is how it happened. Two days ago I had a dramatic encounter with elephants (your elephants) during which I thought that I was in mortal danger more than once. In spite of being very scared I enjoyed the experience, particularly from the safety of hindsight, and I was looking forward to talking about it with someone who I knew would be able to appreciate it. This had to be postponed for technical reasons, and suddenly I realized that I would rather not talk about it and rather keep this very special story to myself. It was as if by talking about it I would somehow lose it. (That is why I prefer not to write about it at this time. It will have to wait until our next meeting.) Our stories and our thoughts are private treasures.

The second observation relates directly to the cost of giving in to the temptation of telling another person about a meaningful experience. It appears that once we tell a story, the way it was told takes precedence over the original version. Then, when we talk or think about it again, we see it the way we told it. There are, however, many different ways to tell a story or to think about one, all of which are lost once we have forced it into the open in a clearly formulated structure. Does this make sense to you? Isn't this the other side of the wisdom to talk about painful experiences? With painful experiences, we want to get rid of them, to some extent, so it is not such a bad idea to talk about them. By the same token, if we want to preserve something we should be very careful not to share it with others too soon.

This might be quite obvious to you, but to someone who has only one important story to tell, and even that only after a long period of drought, it makes a difference. Imagine my dismay when suddenly I heard myself repeating entire phrases that were ready made, waiting to be used again. It was as if language had squeezed the spirit out of the story, leaving only an empty shell.

Best,

Don

P.S. Have you noticed that elephants have exquisite eyelashes?

He couldn't resist the postscript; after all, his therapist is supposed to be the expert on elephants. A small bravado, but since he is "working" until after midnight, he feels that he deserves it. His watch points to one, and before he can do anything about it the letters in "one" start to disintegrate and form the phrase *One New Experience*. Aware of the temptation to use the new "one" for yet another new experience, and so on in infinite regress, he manages to stand up and break the spell. He might have just invented an experiential *perpetuum mobile*, which might enslave him even more than logovory. There are incredible new possibilities in all of this, but he senses the danger and realizes the need for caution.

Sleep doesn't come to him easily, and lying on his back he thinks about the drama of the last two days, and about the importance of keeping it to himself, and about his wish to share it all with Claire. Yes, she is still there, occupying a major part of his existence, permanently in the background of his thoughts. Even when he doesn't think about her she is still there. Would she understand the things that have been happening to him? Would anyone? Would Iris? He tries to recall his feelings when his fingers fumble open the letter. For a while, before he sees who it is from, it could be anything. HIV results—he knows that is unlikely, but if important enough, perhaps not impossible; even Claire, despite the handwriting—if she has changed, maybe her handwriting has as well; Dorothy; Naomi; or even David. He certainly doesn't expect to hear from Iris. The tension before discovering who it's from is very similar to what he felt when his elephant approached the car from behind. Anything is possible. Anything.

✳✳✳✳✳

Five days later, having just finished packing his suitcase, Don takes his cup of tea to the edge of a rock overlooking the game reserve. He is fond of this place and hates to leave, but he can't see any point in staying longer. Instead of driving to Bulawayo again his plan is to return the car in Victoria Falls and catch a flight to Harare. This will give him a chance to drive most of the way inside the park, retracing the way he came. It seems like it's been ages since he was on that bus with the group, and he learns to appreciate the difference of driving alone. At the same time, he has no desire to see the Falls again, as if looking at them with fresh eyes would somehow wipe out his original impressions that have affected him enormously. He is convinced that his discovery concerning storytelling applies to sightseeing as well. He gives himself another hour to take his leave of Sinamatella, hoping the return trip to New York doesn't count as "embarking on a journey." The thought of never returning to this place is simply unbearable. It is another hot day and with the exception of a few scattered oryx and a lonely giraffe, there is no action on the plains below. This makes it easier for Don to replay in his mind the events leading to his decision to go back.

In the waiting room of the HIV unit of the hospital there is a large crowd, and there aren't enough chairs. He is the only white person present, and he feels as if everybody is watching him, although most of the patients—*why "patients," there must be a better word,* he thought—seem to be too absorbed by their own thoughts to care about the others. Looking at each one he tries to guess who is HIV positive. The more people that are found to be positive, the better his chances of not being one of them. Like a quota that has to be met. Like the quotas for the gas chambers in concentration camps. One's hope of surviving depended on others being chosen to die instead. Don knows that in this case it is just a fabrication of his mind, but when he hears the young woman who just entered crying inside the office he can't help himself from thinking that his own chances have improved. It is a long wait, and he is exhausted. He hardly slept at all the night before, waiting for Mwewe to show up at the bar in his hotel. Mwewe doesn't know that he is in town, at least not by ordinary means, and didn't come. He had too many beers, but even that didn't help much, and when he finally got himself to bed he was wide awake and worried. Now, waiting for the verdict that should come any moment, he tries to think about what to do in either scenario.

If he turns out to be infected, he will probably just stay at Sinamatella and try to figure things out. He will have to call Iris, which would be very unpleasant. He will buy himself a lot of books. In his mind he sees himself sitting on his porch with a pile of books and his binoculars, growing weaker and thinner. He needs a decent pen and a few notebooks, just in case. As long as he doesn't need sophisticated medical facilities Sinamatella is probably the best place for him to be. Once his health starts to seriously deteriorate he will have to make some major decisions, but there is plenty of time for that.

And what if he is lucky? The thought itself is intoxicating and turns his head. He will definitely stay some more, and take his time to slowly plan his life. What a luxury that is at his age, to have the opportunity to even think about some kind of a new path. Is this perhaps what Claire needed? Could it be that while he was in his office preparing his clients' tax returns, she was sitting in the kitchen looking off into distance trying to bring some other options into her life? With the children gone, and him remote and preoccupied, what else could she do?

"Mr. Don Mend...Mendelson, this way please." The look on the face of the bespectacled nurse gave no clue as to what she might know. His heart races so fast now that he can feel it pounding against his chest, beneath his left breast pocket. The letter from Iris, neatly folded, is still there. The nurse motions him to sit down, and it scares him even more. She looks at some paper on her desk and smiles for the first time.

"Mr. Mendelson, I have good news for you. Your tests were negative. I hope you now realize the need for precautions in the future." Don takes a deep breath and nods his head in vigorous agreement. "If at some time you experience another episode of unprotected sex, be sure to wait at least two months before taking the test. The immunological markers take time to develop, and we have no way today of measuring a person's current status." After a short while she smiles again and adds, "In any event, you can rest assured that until two months ago you were free of the virus."

Don can't remember how he left the hospital, drove to his hotel, paid the bill, and started his long drive back. It is only when the by now familiar scenery of the dry country makes an impact on his brain that he can focus properly. The test was in vain, the worry, the waiting, everything was in vain. In fact, for all he knows he might still be infected with the virus, but he will have to wait at least another month to take a second test, and then another week to get the results. There is no way he can be expected to do that. No way. Sinamatella is good for someone who is HIV positive, or negative for that matter, but it isn't so good for someone waiting to find out. Too much free time. What he needs now is to get busy. So busy that he won't find time to think. There is only one place where he can do that, and that is his office in New York. Immersing himself in the pile of papers that have been accumulating on his desk since he left is just the thing for him to do. He will surround himself with documents, and drown his thoughts in the process. It isn't what he had planned. It isn't what he had hoped for. Not at all. But it is, after all, an emergency. A real, proper *em-er-g-en-cy*. He tries to let the word fly ahead of him hoping that it will disintegrate into its constituent letters that will then sprout into new meanings, but nothing happens. *I'm too tired,* he thought. *Just too tired.*

The oryx move slowly toward the river to drink, but the giraffe is nowhere to be seen. He must have missed her moving into the forest. There are few things as beautiful as a giraffe gliding across a landscape, and he is sorry that he is so preoccupied that he missed that. He tries the binoculars, searching the tops of the acacia trees in the hope of catching a glimpse of the long neck and the beautiful eyes. At some point he thinks he has her, but it is too far to be sure.

Trophies

It is the taxi drive from JFK to Manhattan that finally brings him back to his new reality. He can't remember how long he has been in transit, or exactly what the date is, but during the flight itself he didn't mind. High above the clouds the sun looks just like it does in Africa. The fatigue had caught up with him while he was waiting for his luggage. His suitcase was among the last to arrive, and he was convinced that it had been misplaced and sent somewhere else. The cab driver suggests taking the long route via Triborough Bridge since there is construction on the LIE and it's jammed. He has a heavy foreign accent and Don doesn't trust him. He insists on taking the LIE. After all, he is an experienced New Yorker, and nobody is going to take advantage of him. The driver shrugs his shoulders and keeps silent. Don realizes that in the absence of confirmation he will need to closely watch the road. He is tense and irritated. For a while traffic seems to be alright, but then they hit the jam about two miles before the Midtown Tunnel. He sees the driver smiling to himself, trying to catch his eyes in the mirror. Don feels foolish and totally exhausted. He needs a shower and he needs some sleep. It is only five in the afternoon and he will have to stretch the evening for as long as possible or else he will wake up in the middle of the night. Zimbabwe is six hours ahead of New York, and his biological clock reads midnight. He wishes it was midnight now and he wishes he was in his lodge at Sinamatella. And how exactly is he supposed to stretch the evening? Should he call Naomi? Perhaps talk with Carl and find out what is happening at the firm? He doesn't feel like calling anybody and almost hopes that the traffic jam will solve the problem for him.

In spite of the abruptness of his decision to return, he has great plans for himself. Clearly he is not the same person who left New York just over a month ago, and he means to make sure that everything he gained is well protected from the wear and tear of this city. Nothing will be the same again, nothing. Even his return to work will be only temporary, before he finds a way to sell his company to Carl, or anybody who will buy it. He knows that for the time being he should keep his plans to himself. Even Dorothy must not know, or he will lose his grip on the firm. She should seriously think of retiring too. He recalls having this thought on several occasions prior to his trip. It worries him to witness his memory trying to establish ties to his old self. Is there a way to resist this? He will have to figure it out.

The cab driver is fighting his way through the traffic jam, constantly switching lanes. It seems to Don that each time he moves to another lane the old one makes better progress. Is he doing it out of spite? It is a clear day, and the panoramic Manhattan skyline is well defined. The tall buildings remind him of the horns of an oryx. No, they are not spiked enough for that. The Empire State Building is especially appropriate for the horn comparison, but there are no unicorns in Africa. Close to the toll plaza the forward movement stops altogether. There is a constant stream of cars from the side that manage to position themselves in front of his cab, and he hates them. *The driver is too passive,* he thought. *Come on, this is New York! Unless you block the others we will never get anywhere. There is enough room to squeeze by, even elephants know that.* The driver of a huge van in front of them must have realized that he needs the other lane and starts to back up. Don wonders if wishing him to stop will make any difference, but he's too tired to concentrate. Realizing that so many things remind him of his venture in Africa is a comfort. He feels as if he is literally carrying the last month with him, well packed in the folds of his brain. It is a heavy and rich load, and he has managed to import it without paying customs. In fact, just by looking at him nobody suspects that he is bringing in valuable stuff.

He tries to imagine the customs official asking, "Do you have anything to declare?"

"Yes, previous thoughts and memories."

"How much did you pay for them?"

"A great deal. I lost my wife."

"Let me check. Where do you keep them?"

"In my brain."

"Let me have a look."

At this point his driver asks if he can have money for the toll, and instead of being subjected to a thorough search of his brain, Don searches his pockets. After removing some Zimbabwe dollars and a few British pounds he manages to find a twenty dollar bill. However, this won't do, and after dismissing it the driver uses his own money. Why doesn't he pay himself in the first place? From a purely economic viewpoint the driver should always prefer to pay for the toll, since it may increase the tip. True, this will work only if the tip is a percentage of the total, but he knows that to be the case. He is the professional CPA now. There is no reason to disavow his past, and even if he had wanted to he wouldn't know how to go about it. It too is part of the same baggage he permanently carries in the folds of his brain. Even Claire is inside him. He has only lied to the custom official about losing her. You can't lose anything or anybody once they have been stored there. But it is the real Claire that he wants now, and the idea that as soon as he gets out of the tunnel they will both share the same small island in the Atlantic Ocean is potent with possibilities. He has never before thought of Manhattan as a small island in the Atlantic Ocean, but it is, of course, just that.

On such a small island anything can happen. He might run into her at the Lincoln Center, at MOMA, or even at the Guggenheim, although he has never been particularly interested in museums. He might be doing a little shopping at Zabar's and boom, there's Claire in the same isle. There are so many possibilities for them to meet that it is in fact quite strange that it hasn't happened several times already. He feels fortunate that they haven't met yet, since he wasn't ready for it. *It is pure luck,* he thought. Things have changed now, and he was confident that they are destined to meet soon. Coincidence? Given what he has learned from Mwewe, there is no such thing as a simple coincidence. Claire and he will be inevitably drawn across Manhattan to the same place at the same time. Just as the cab is emerging from the tunnel Don imagines two lines crisscrossing New York, at first each pursuing its own autonomous course, and then some powerful force altering their directions and bringing them together. Don knows that unless the two lines actually merge into one, their point of contact must be infinitesimally small, the brief time represented by a dot. From there it is separation again.

It is difficult for two adults to merge, unless one of them swallows the other, he thought. *They should be just close enough to feel the other's presence without actually touching. Like two heavenly bodies in orbit, hurling their gravity at each other across space. Could it be that the ancient Greeks were right and the planets had love affairs? With thoughts like this I must be becoming a poet or something. It is pleasant to have such thoughts. Now that I have them I must cultivate them. Perhaps I should write them down. Perhaps I should keep a notebook with me at all times.*

The first thing he notices when he enters his apartment is the familiar smell. He finds it odd that it is just the way he left it, as if he has expected everything to change. As far as he's concerned, the place has always been too big, even when the children were at home. Now, after Africa, it is huge, and clearly unnecessary. It is an old building with high ceilings, and much too expensive to heat in the winter. It was Claire's choice, and for years she took loving care of the smallest details. Flowers were her specialty, and they were the first casualties after she left. Sitting dejected on the sofa next to his luggage Don realizes that he should get some flowers to liven the place up. *It can use vacuuming as well,* he thought. *And it needs fresh air. And air conditioning.*

"Home is the sailor, home from the sea, and the hunter home from the hill." He wasn't sure whether the quote is correct, but he likes the sound of it. There is of course no beer in the refrigerator and he adds it to his mental list of things to do. Then he opens the window and makes a brief call to Dr. Irving Hunt, arranging an appointment for the day after tomorrow. Then he takes a long shower, makes himself a cup of coffee, and comfortably wrapped in the robe that Claire chose for one of his birthdays, he sifts through his mail. It is mostly junk mail, and he throws it away without opening the bulky envelopes. This is new for him, for in the past he couldn't throw away anything without checking it out first. The movement itself is pleasant and suggests freedom. It is as if by resisting the temptation to open the envelopes he demonstrates some kind of superiority. In some cases it is ambiguous whether he can throw the stuff away without looking, and he dares not take a chance. He hates those, since they show him that yes, he is liberated, but only to a point. *Maybe I returned too soon,* he thought. *Maybe I'm not ready yet.* But he is too tired to let systematic remorse take hold of him. That will have to wait until tomorrow morning.

He calls Naomi in Louisville but gets her voicemail instead. He leaves a message for her to call him back and immediately realizes that it is a mistake. Now he is caught, and he can't go to sleep. Should he take the phone off the hook? No, she might be worried. Not only does he suddenly materialize, but on top of this surprise he also can't be reached. Sounds like a heart attack or a stroke. Although he hasn't watched TV for more than a month, there is nothing that can keep his attention from wondering, and several times he finds himself falling asleep. After some more struggle he gives up and goes to bed. The bed is too large, and he makes sure to lie exclusively on his side. The monotonous hum of the air conditioner keeps the street noise at bay, and it looks like he will easily fall asleep, if not for the vision of Claire that hovers beyond his eyelids more clearly than usual. He sees her emerging from the bathroom in her white robe, her black hair well brushed and hanging loosely over her shoulders. He is waiting for her to discard the robe and join him in bed, but she just stands there looking down at him. It is a look of pity, and he can't stand it. Suddenly he is wide awake, switches on the light, and tries to read one of the issues of

Time that was in the mailbox. The troubles of the world gradually push Claire out of his consciousness, and he falls asleep with the light on.

The phone must have been ringing several times before he manages to tear himself from deep oblivion into wakefulness. He looks at his watch, and sees that it is eleven. He has slept for barely one hour. The phone feels heavy in his hand, and he coughs twice to prepare himself for what is to come.

"Hi, Daddy. I hope I didn't wake you up."

"Oh, no, it's OK."

"Are you sure? You sound sleepy."

"It's fine, daughter. How have you been? It has been quite a while since we talked."

"When did you come back?"

"Just a few hours ago."

"I'm sorry for calling so late. You must be tired. But I was so glad to hear your voice that I couldn't resist calling you right away. How are you, Daddy?"

"I'm great, daughter. I missed you a lot."

"I missed you too. Did you have a good time?"

"I had a great time. I will tell you more when we see each other. When does your semester end?"

"It ended already, but I have some papers to write, and I plan to stay here for most of the summer."

"Good...good."

"You're not angry with me, are you?"

"Of course not. Why should I be?"

"I mean for not coming, and for not being with you all this time."

"Naomi, you have your own life to live. And please don't worry about me, I'm fine."

"I didn't expect you to return yet. Is everything alright?"

"I didn't expect it either, but don't worry, everything is alright."

"Does Mother know that you're back?"

"No, of course not."

"Do you want me to tell her?"

Don doesn't know what to say, and there is a long pause.

"Should I call her and tell her? You can be honest with me."

"I see that you've grown up, and I'm very happy for you."

"Thanks, Daddy. And I won't tell her unless you ask me to."

"Have you heard anything from David?"

"No, not since Passover."

"I see."

"I did speak with Mother, though."

"Yes?"

"Yes, when I got your letter from Africa."

"I see."

"You should have heard the surprise in her voice. She was totally unprepared for anything like that."

"I see."

"I'm so glad for you. And you must tell me all about it."

"I will, but not on the phone."

"I understand."

"Thank you for calling, and goodnight."

"Goodnight, Daddy."

The banal conversation leaves him unsatisfied. There are so many things he would like to share with her, but not of the type that could be shared during a long-distance call. He knows that the opportunities for establishing even a limited intimacy between them are long past, and he wonders whether Naomi feels the same deep loss that he now feels. *She grew up too quickly,* he thought. *Only yesterday she was a child, and now she is a young woman on her own, with nothing in between to warn me. Like my own abandonment. Like my sudden departure from Africa. Everything is too abrupt. Time is playing some dirty tricks, out of spite. Like a hyena,* he thought.

✳✳✳✳✳

The next morning, sitting at his well-polished and empty desk, Don doesn't expect to have so little mail waiting for him at the office; between Carl and Dorothy things seem to be better under control than he had anticipated. It somehow spoils his unannounced reentry into the life of Mendelson & Stewart, Inc., CPAs, although on the few occasions that he thought about it in Africa he had predicted and hoped for just this situation. He is quickly discovering that things look and feel very different from here. *They are both genuinely glad to see me back here,* he thought, *but at the same time they didn't know what to make of it, and I'm in no position to explain.* In some respects they are probably still trying to understand his decision to stay in Africa, and now on top of that there is this sudden one-eighty of events. Who knows what he might do next? It is the last thing one would expect from the senior partner at any respectable company. For a CPA it is definitely unusual.

From their viewpoint, what started as an obvious attempt to recuperate from his troubles turned into something that they couldn't possibly comprehend. Certainly not after his cable about transferring the money, which it now turns out he doesn't need. Don can't help himself and calculates how much he lost in the transaction. While he was there, that too seemed entirely inconsequential. For a few critical seconds he fights the need to make use of such a special word like "inconsequential," and just when he's about to give up despite telling himself "DON'T," he realizes that "DON'T" is made of *DON* plus *T.* Although he doesn't know what to make of it, his attention is sufficiently diverted from the minefield of logovory.

Instead, he sent *DON* gliding into the light space ahead of him, watching the letters dispersing in all directions and then coming together as new words. *Dwell On Nothingness,* he read, all the time knowing that he just made it up. *Dwell on nothingness! What an odd message. How am I supposed to dwell on nothingness? It sounds like some cheap Buddhist slogan. And yet, of all the things that I could have come up with for the letter N, why did I come up with nothingness? Could have been* numbers, news, New York, nature, neurosis, *even* Naomi. *There must be hundreds of things starting with N that I can dwell on if I have to. In fact, of all the possible things,* nothingness *would be the last I wish to dwell on, although at this moment sitting in this office that has known both better and worse times, it wouldn't be entirely inappropriate.*

There is nothing for me to do in this office. Not today, not tomorrow, not ever. I should sell and move out from this profession as soon as possible, before it sucks me back into my discarded shell. What is a CPA after all? It is a Continuous Paper Agony, *that is what it is! Should I wait until it's too late only to discover like old Prufrock, who measured his life in coffee spoon, that I have measured mine in paper? My needs are minimal. I don't care much for fancy restaurants, nor do I need a fancy car. What I need is food and transportation. Let me just make a brief calculation…assuming that I leave this job and don't take on another one, how much money would I need to get by?*

Don is now getting excited. It has been years since he read T.S. Eliot, and the sudden emergence of Prufrock is a precious novelty. He opens his new legal pad and starts writing in quick, nervous strokes. After a short while he tears the paper from the pad, crumples it, and throws it in the wastebasket. On a new page he tries to arrange his thoughts more systematically.

Monthly expenses: $2,500(1)

Annual expenses: $30,000

1 Excluding onetime major expenses. Also pending the needs of the children and Claire. Plus expenses for therapy. Plus medical insurance.

Assuming six percent interest on CDs, I would need half a million. The apartment alone is probably worth that much, but if and when Claire files for divorce she will be entitled to half of that. My Keogh and IRAs will only become available seven years from now, so that's out. Currently available assets: $250,000, mostly in long-term bonds. I should keep those for a rainy day. That means that if I don't want to sell the apartment—in which case I will have to buy something else instead—my shares in the firm should be sold for at least half a million. Are they worth it?

Don knows that the revenue of Mendelson & Stewart, Inc., was close to two million dollars last year, and their net after tax profit (excluding salaries) was $120,000. Thus, the company could easily be worth one million, and his sixty percent share is worth at least $600,000. The location of the company in the downtown financial district is superb and business is good. With some luck, he might pull it off. But luck isn't his strong suit, and he feels caught. Unless…unless he leaves for Africa where life is so much cheaper, and rents out his New York apartment. That should bring him $2,000 per month after tax, which should be just enough to cover his expenses there.

He suspects that this *Dwelling On Numbers* is premature, but it gives him a sense of being practical, another thing that isn't his strong suit. Lately, however, he thinks that his performance on practical matters hasn't been so bad. He managed quite well on his own in Africa. Life there is so much simpler. He is aware of his tendency to get carried away by numbers, and they will probably look very different in a few days. He should bide his time.

Meanwhile, he can introduce some changes into his office that were long overdue. There are four enlarged photos he found in the small duty free shop in Harare, which he now removes from his briefcase and spreads on his large desk. The drinking elephant is a large bull standing alone by a waterhole. With the exception of a few small shrubs, the entire landscape is empty, further magnifying the majestic creature that appears totally absorbed by drinking. Don can almost see the slow movement that preceded the still picture. It consists of a gentle heave of the trunk, followed by an almost imperceptible lowering of the massive head. He put the lioness with her three cubs next to the elephant. She is lying on her back, and the cubs are trampling all over her. For obvious reasons he would have preferred a lioness by herself, but the tourist shop didn't have one. Above her he puts the golden red rocks of the Matopos. A place he missed out on and thinks about a lot. Can it be that unseen places have as much influence as familiar ones? The rock formation is unlike anything he has seen and he wonders whether that is the place where Mwewe spent the night, and whether he will ever see him again. And then there is the baobab tree. None of the pictures of the Victoria Falls do any justice to the real thing and he preferred to skip them, but when he came across this tree he felt a compulsion to look and look again, and there was no way he could leave the shop without taking it with him. It is an ordinary baobab, if there are any ordinary baobabs. Nothing like the enormous tree above Hwange that scared him away. The picture was taken during the dry season and the short, naked branches are perfectly silhouetted against an afternoon sky. The trunk is very wide and its surface is so smooth that in some spots it actually reflects the strong African light. There is an enormous power emanating from the trunk of that tree sprouting in all directions. Even here, in the safety of his office, Don doesn't feel comfortable with it. It is difficult to stop looking at it, and its impact isn't pleasant. He can't understand what it is about the tree that disturbs him so, and he decides that if he hangs it in his office or in his apartment he will be putting himself in jeopardy. That settles it; the tree must go. It will be a good present for Irv, instead of the elephant.

Removing the IRS regulations from the shelves facing his desk is, he thinks, a great thing to do on the morning of his return. He arranges them in the corner on top of each other and puts the elephant and the Matopos in their place. From where he sits, all he has to do is slightly lift his gaze and there they are, his trophies. *My small, but perhaps well-deserved spiritual trophies,* he thought, and he is immediately overwhelmed with the desire to show them to Claire. She hates his office, and for the first time he can see it through her eyes.

$Baobab$

The next afternoon Don can hardly wait to see Irv. There are so many things he wants to tell him that at one point he prepared a list to make sure that he wouldn't forget anything. *That in itself is major progress,* he thought, *since in the past I worried that I would go and there would be nothing to talk about.* It is a long list, and each word represents a complex set of experiences. There is no way they can go over it during the standard fifty-minute session:

> *Elephants*
> *Iris*
> *Mwewe*
> *HIV*

Baobab?

Logovory and acronymy

CPA?

In the end, all of this planning turns out irrelevant, since the exchange between patient and therapist follows an entirely different route. "You look good," says Irv at the entrance to his office.

"Thank you, I feel good." Don wonders why the need for the "thank you," although in this case it is not entirely unjustified. Before taking his usual seat he moves a few steps closer to the elephants and looks at them very carefully. Having spent so much time in this room before, he is struck by how different they look to him now. "I have an elephant story for you," he says. "It is quite a remarkable elephant story."

Irv looks interested but motions him to sit down and get back to their routine. Don doesn't want to get back to their routine as if nothing has happened since he left here, but in the meantime his story will have to wait for the right moment. The picture of the baobab that he brought with him will also have to wait. He plans to use it to illustrate a point, and he doesn't want to waste it. Once properly seated, Irv gives him a long and searching look.

In his own mind Don thinks of himself as practically cured, but there is something in this room that pushes him toward a more cautious evaluation. *Could it be pure habit? I must ask him about it, because if there is such a thing, in order to actually feel better patients would always need to eventually move to new surroundings. One cannot be expected to rant about one's feelings in the same room where for months on end all one ever felt was negative. Maybe it's a trick that guarantees the need for long treatments.* Don doesn't know what has come over him; he doesn't want to think this kind of mean thoughts. Today he is eager to share his experiences with the person who sent him on this voyage and instead, he is mean and suspicious. *Think of Mwewe,* he told himself. *Think of his long trip to Sinamatella just to briefly see a newfound friend.*

"Was it a good trip for you?"

"Yes, exactly what I needed. Thanks for making me take it."

"And what brought you back?"

"It's a long story."

"Tell me. Tell me all about it."

And so Don finds himself describing his two nights with Iris and how they came about, and the subsequent worry about AIDS, the test he took, the difficult period of waiting for the results, and the futility of the entire enterprise.

"There was just no way I could stay there for six more weeks worrying about it. I needed something to do in the meantime, and I hope that the office will supply that. However, I was probably wrong, since there isn't much to do there, at least not yet."

"What you are saying is that you left Africa in the hope of finding the solution to your worries here in New York?"

Don doesn't like the way it has been phrased, but he has to agree just the same. "Yes, but only for a short while."

"You mean until you get the test results?"

"Yes. No, only until I find a buyer for my company." He realizes that it is unrelated to the previous argument and must sound crazy, but now that it is in the open he doesn't mind. Dealing with inconsistencies is, after all, one of the simplest things that his therapist is supposed to do. Irv is getting good money for his effort, so why not make use of it? Sure, it was bizarre if not outright insane to leave an organized tour and decide to stay in the middle of nowhere by himself, only to suddenly come back, and just as quickly to decide to go back to Africa for good. What's happening to him? Are these the signs of being cured? Signs of an impending nervous breakdown would be more like it. In his mind he can see himself being caught in endless travel between New York and Harare, with barely enough time to get to Sinamatella before his next flight back. If the back and forth movement is fast enough, he may actually be suspended in the air somewhere above the Atlantic. Like being squeezed in the narrow bottleneck of the coffee maker acting like a light-filled hourglass lying on its side. His headache, which he attributes to jet lag, is intensifying, and he feels the growing pressure in his temples. Irv must have sensed something, because he asks him if he is alright.

"Yes. Just a little confused, that's all. Nothing serious." *How unfair*, he thought. *How totally unfair. The proud hunter, home from the hill, suddenly finding himself the object of pity and ridicule.*

"Is your mind elsewhere? Struggling with words?"

"Not so much lately, and not in the same way as before. Instead of cutting them into pieces I now use them as raw materials to create new meanings. Acronymy, I call it. Occasionally I still feel the compulsion for logovory, but acronymy is gradually taking over."

"What is it that you actually do?"

"I take a word and send it on a trip ahead of me and watch it disintegrate into letters and then come back together again, with each letter standing for a new word."

"Can you give me an example?"

"Sure. Take HIV. It comes back as *Hoping In Vain*. It could be anything, only it isn't."

"How did it start?"

Don tells him about the dream, and he's aware of putting too much emphasis on the bottleneck.

"What do you see when the letters become words?"

"I don't always see this happening, but sometimes it looks like the words are sprouting from the letters. Like the branches from the trunk of a tree…that reminds me, I brought you a small present."

"A baobab tree! Aren't they wonderful? I love baobabs. Thanks, I will find a good spot for it somewhere among the elephants."

"It scared me, for some reason. I mean, the tree actually scared me."

"Can you think of a possible reason?"

"No. But I think that it has something to do with the dream, and with this new way of obsessing about words."

"Do you enjoy this acronymy of yours?"

"Yes, it's a lot of fun, and I can learn something from it. The new words come without any effort, like some messages from within. They tell me things about myself that I wouldn't otherwise know. You might say that they are coming from the unconscious."

"Shall we try some more? Are you up for it?"

"Sure. Give me a word."

"How about 'Claire'?"

"*Cutting Language And Inventing Reasonable Expressions.*" It is quick and effortless. *And relevant,* he thought.

"But that has nothing to do with her, does it?"

"How should I know? Perhaps it does. Perhaps everything I do has something to do with her?"

"You may be right. Want to try some more?"

"Go ahead."

"Let's try 'Claire' once more."

Don sends her name gently ahead of him, and this time it takes a bit longer before she comes back as *Costly Love As Irrevocably Risky Emotion.*

"Don."

"That's easy: *Dwell On Nothingness.* But that was cheating, since I've done that one once before."

"Can you make any sense of it?"

"No, I can't."

"Why don't you work on it as homework? Would you?"

It has been some time since Irv gave him homework, and it further emphasizes to him how far he still has to go. But he is grateful to him for not probing into his confused decision to sell and leave. For reasons of his own he has left that entire area untouched throughout their session, despite Don's obvious invitation. He knows, however, that its time will come. He has a pounding headache and outside it is hot and humid. Quickly, a cab home.

Late that evening Irv searches his library for information about automatic writing. In an old volume on hypnoanalysis he reads, "Automatic writing is a splendid means of gaining access to unconscious material that lies beyond the grasp of conscious recall. The portion of the cerebrum that controls the automatic writing seems to have access to material unavailable to the centers that control speech." And later on, when describing the actual product, the characterization reads, "Automatic writing is subject to the same distortions and disguises as dreams. Condensations, phonetic spelling, punning, literary allusions, and fragmentation of sentences and words are common. *Single letters may stand for words* and numbers, and peculiar symbols may indicate words and ideas." That is exactly what he is looking for. Even though he has never used automatic writing as a therapeutic tool, when Don described acronymy, he suspected that the two were somehow related. It was the apparent ease with which he came up with the new phrases that raised Irv's suspicion that the action was to some extent automatic. He is very excited because out of the blue his patient has come up with a device that gives him the perfect means of studying his most secret thoughts and wishes. *Better even than dreams,* he thought, *and no need for hypnosis.* Here is a true "royal road" to the unconscious.

The homework, thought Don, *is impossible.* He has in fact been asked to dwell on dwelling on nothingness, a task without a natural beginning, no clue, and no idea to start from. It is not for lack of trying, for he has learned to take Irv's assignments seriously. They have worked for him in the past, at least most of them, but this time seems different. What is the best environment for this type of homework? Is he supposed to sit in the lotus position and contemplate his navel? For as long as he could remember Don has been opposed to anything having to do with Eastern tradition. Despite its limitations, and he is now perhaps more sensitive to those limitations than ever before, he prefers Western rationality to the fuzzy notions associated with the East. Consequently, instead of assuming the yogi position he sits himself comfortably in front of the TV and flips through the channels. He opens a pack of unshelled walnuts and immerses himself in the task of breaking, shelling, and eating. Walnuts are his favorite mostly because he likes to crack them by pressing two against each other in his palm, until the weaker one gives way. It is one of the few things he learned from his father, and one of the few things he taught David. If the nuts are not fresh it requires a lot of strength to crack them this way. Sometimes it doesn't work at all. He likes it most when the walnuts crack into two symmetrical halves, looking very much like the two hemispheres of the human brain. In those instances additional pressure is needed to extract the nut from its protective shell. He sees himself as an ancient hunter breaking human skulls with his bare hands. Alternatively, his approach attempts to extract the innermost secrets from the brain, chew them properly, and then swallow. For while he watches women's tennis and the heap of shells on the table grows steadily.

The tennis is excellent, and the match is going to be decided by a tiebreaker. *There is something basically unfair,* he thought, *in a situation where so much depends on a few swings. It is unfair, but very exciting.* By then he is down to two walnuts, and they are particularly difficult to crack. Finally, with both palms sore from exertion, he hears the crack and proceeds to extract the nut. The tiebreaker is reaching a particularly tense moment, and it takes him a few seconds to realize that the nut is stale and bitter. Once the taste registers he runs to the bathroom and spits it out. It is the first rotten walnut he has come across, and he needs to crack the remaining one fast, to overcome the bitter taste. However, his system requires at least two walnuts, and he can't open this one without the necessary counter pressure. The player that he favors to win is now down seven-six, and in spite of the lingering bitter taste he doesn't dare leave the TV to search for a solution to his problem. She double faults on her last serve and loses the match in the most frustrating way. Disgusted, he searches and finds a nutcracker, and he cracks the last skull with the help of technology, only to discover that the last nut is rotten as well. Still unbelieving, he pours himself some Budweiser and wonders what the chances are of two rotten nuts, out of a pile of perhaps sixty or more, to end up together as the last pair? What can this mean? Is it perhaps the risk of trying to extract the brain's secrets? *I may find them at the end to be too bitter to swallow?* he thought, *Or are the two rotten nuts the perfect match to the last faults in the tennis match? Another coincidence? And the matching of the two words, is that yet another coincidence? What is happening to me? Have I become the creator of coincidences? The meeting ground of unrelated events waiting to be granted some meaning? What is a coincidence anyway? It is first and foremost a* coi-nc-i-de-nce. *No, I don't want to do this now, I have homework to do. Why waste time on logovory instead of dwelling on nothingness? Unless they are one and the same thing. Unless logovory is an attempt to dwell on nothingness! Well, not really to dwell on it, but rather engage in it so there would be no chance to dwell on it. A preventive maneuver. Homework finished.*

The next day Irv doesn't waste any time, and as soon as they sit down he moves straight to the point: "So, did you think about our last meeting?"

"Sure."

"And what did you come up with?"

"I think that this thing with nothingness is related to my symptoms. I mean, to logovory."

"In what way?"

"Could it be that its main purpose is to force me to be continuously preoccupied with actions that prevent me from thinking? From facing nothingness?"

"Oh, yes, very much so! But why? What is it that frightens you so much? This tremendous investment in self-distraction, what is it distracting you from?"

"I wish I knew," Don says, immediately realizing that for years now he has been doing everything in his power to prevent himself from knowing. "It's as if this nothingness actually exists, and it must be avoided at all costs."

Irv is obviously pleased and wants to make the most of this latest breakthrough. It is important to find out as much as possible about the potential link between an idea and the symptom, and he presses the point further. "When did you have this insight? How did it come about?"

"It was while I was watching tennis, not really watching but just looking, while at the same time I tried to do my homework without knowing how to go about it. I became bothered by all these coincidences converging on me as if I were some kind of lightning rod or something, and suddenly there were so many of them that I had to escape. The way I tried to escape was by taking the word *coincidence* and cutting it into pieces. Lately I haven't been doing this as often, and I felt bad about it, since I should have been thinking of nothingness instead, and the next thing I knew, the two were connected."

Irv recalls his own thoughts about the possible function of his patient's symptoms, but it is now obvious that as is often the case, they serve more than one function. Although very direct in other aspects of therapy, he rarely actively encourages his patients to talk about the meaning of their symptoms. This time, however, is an exception.

"In your mind, what is logovory like? What does it remind you of? Now that you seem to be somewhat less bothered by it than before, and especially since you are gaining these valuable insights into it, try to take a step back from it and tell me what it's like."

Don's gaze suddenly rests on the baobab nestling between two pictures of elephants, and he quickly closes his eyes. He tries to imagine the task of logovory but finds it hard without an actual word to work on. So he takes *bao-bab* as his raw material, but it's too easy.

"Phenomenologically"—*now, that is a word!* Don thought— "there are three distinct phases to the operation. First, there is the strong urge to do it." Now that he has started speaking, Don opens his eyes and looks at his therapist. "Something signaling that if I start with it I would know exactly how to proceed, and that the next few seconds will be filled with activity at which I am very proficient, a true professional. Then, once I commit myself to do it, there is a brief moment of planning the cut, then the cutting itself, and finally, the satisfaction in discovering the precise center."

Irv recalls his notes on *Homo symmetricus* and wants to know more about this particular satisfaction.

"It is like when you do a neurological test and even with your eyes closed the finger finds the tip of your nose," Don explains.

"The nose is your center?"

"Yes, and so is the navel. Maybe that's why Buddha was so enthralled by it."

"What else?"

"Dividing goodies between my two children. If you don't know the exact number of goodies in a pile you have no way to ensure equity, unless you do it piecemeal. Whenever it was an odd number, I used to take the remaining treat myself, for the sake of fairness…I see Solomon sitting in judgment threatening to divide a child in half for the same reason. It looks familiar, I must have dreamed it, or perhaps I saw a painting of it."

"What else?"

"Plenty. I now have several images all relating to the discovery of the center. I see a herd of elephants, and try to locate the matriarch…I am canoeing with Claire and aim for the inverted *V* to ensure proper passage…then there is the search for balance, the "ego" you would call it—isn't the ego in your theories supposed to be located somewhere in the center?"

Irv nods his head, but realizing that Don is just warming up to something, he doesn't speak.

"Yes. And there is this inverted *V* again, but this time not in the river, but standing up like a perfectly symmetrical hill, you know, the type that children draw. First you climb up, then you reach the summit, and from there it is all downhill."

"Like the midpoint of one's life?"

"Yes. Once you pass it, it is all downhill. Like Prufrock."

Irv is very proud of his patient, who, in addition to being *Homo symmetricus* and *Homo dysinfectus,* has now showed himself to be *Homo existencialis* as well. He has a clear preference for people who are preoccupied with old age and death, something that he considers elementary in adulthood. "Worried about time?"

"Of course, aren't you?"

"Were you always worried about time?"

"I don't remember being worried before—I mean, before Claire left—but perhaps I was, without realizing it. Do you think she might have left because she was worried about time?"

"Do you think she might have?"

By now Don is used to the fact that Irv avoids answering questions and almost automatically turns them around as new stimuli to his patient. At first it had disturbed him, but not anymore.

"Yes, certainly she could have. You see, I was so boring, and with the children gone, nothing new ever happened in our lives. That gave her a lot of time to think about how she was wasting her life with me. It was the routine that drove her crazy. I should have known better, but I was too scared to let go of routine. On the contrary, I used to pride myself in routinizing everything. Like the Japanese, I think. Turning life into a well-stylized tea ceremony."

"How do you feel about it now?"

"Now is different. Things have happened. Everything is in a constant flux, and I have a hard time stopping to take a closer look. It's as if the ice inside me is melting and I am slowly warming up, without knowing what to expect. But Mwewe, my African friend, was right—I started on a journey from which there was no turning back. Not even if I have to act like a lightning rod for all these coincidences that make no sense to me. I have no idea what is it that is being defrosted, but it certainly doesn't feel like nothingness."

At this point Don's gaze falls once more on the baobab, but he is not scared anymore, and pointing to it with his fully outstretched left arm he goes on, "And I think I know what it was about that tree that frightened me so much. It was its energy. The thick trunk filled with reserves of moisture and vitality, sending new life in all directions. I couldn't bear looking at it, feeling so empty inside. Empty and dead."

Irv isn't one to be easily impressed, but he is seeing Don with new eyes now. Where has all this come from? He would like to attribute the success to himself, but he knows that only a small share of it is his. He is curious about the rest, but that will have to wait.

"And now you have acronymy sprouting from within, giving life to new thoughts and ideas?"

It is now Don's turn to look admiringly at his therapist before responding: "Yes, that's exactly right."

Cemetery

The phone call from Claire is no coincidence, but subsequently Don wonders whether its impossible timing wasn't one. He has just come back from the supermarket carrying four heavy bags, and before organizing the stuff he needs to go to the bathroom. It is just before he can relieve himself that he hears the phone ringing. Once, twice, three times…and without being able to pull up his pants in time he runs to pick it up. He could never understand people who let the phone ring while they are home without answering. It signifies willpower that is beyond his meager resources, and he is full of admiration. On this occasion his urgency for the bathroom is so great that he almost manages to stay put, but the phone in his home never rings anymore,

---

the answering machine is off, and he just can't let it go. The blinds are open and he worries that a neighbor might see him.

The assault, however, comes from the phone itself. It has been a long time since he heard Claire's voice, and as on all previous occasions since her departure, the jolt it gives him is automatic. In return to her brief, "Hello, Don?" he gasps, catches his breath, and the "Hello, Claire" comes out just a little too late. For years she had insisted that the common "Hi" was too vulgar, and the entire family was expected to use the more formal greeting. Although perfectly aware of the privacy of his embarrassing situation, Claire's voice brings her so close that Don feels exposed and vulnerable. At the same time, the excitement is potent enough to surface above its disconcerting context.

"Is this a good time to talk?"

She must have sensed something already. Sensitivity is certainly one of Claire's strong points. Perhaps too strong.

"Yes, this is a good time," he says, his left hand still fumbling with his zipper, aware of using her words, unable to think.

"I didn't know if you were back from Africa, but I had a hunch that you were, so I tried my luck." Don wonders where this hunch has come from. Since when has Claire been capable of such a Mwewe-esque feat? And tuned to him, of all people? Naomi probably told her after all. But still, being able to sense her mood he immediately realizes that she sounds genuinely glad to have reached him, and he likes the way she enunciates "Africa." It is very soft, not unlike the way the word is pronounced by most Africans.

"I was just coming home with some groceries when I heard the phone and almost missed you." Why the lie? And why not say she had almost missed him? *Take care, Don, take care.*

"It's good to hear your voice. When did you return?"

"A few days ago."

"Is everything alright? I mean, was it planned?" Definitely Naomi.

"Everything is fine. How about you?"

"Oh, I'm great, really. Very busy, but great. I started working some time ago."

"What do you do?"

"Mainly editing."

"Yes? How odd."

"Why odd? Don't you remember that I always sort of toyed with the idea of working with language?"

"Yes, I certainly remember. Still, it is odd that both of us should be engaged in the same thing." Stupid, watch your tongue!

"I don't understand. What do you mean both of us do the same thing?"

"It's a long story, but I do a lot of word processing myself. I'll tell you about it sometime."

"I didn't know that. Yes, you should tell me about it sometime. Which reminds me, do you think you could come to the cemetery on Friday? I know that you don't think much of these occasions, but it will be the tenth anniversary of my mother's death. It's hard to believe how fast time flies."

Yes, Don thought, *it is hard to believe that more than six months have gone by since I've seen Claire.* Six months, and two or three weeks, he wasn't sure. Until recently he had known to the exact day, but at some point during his stay in Sinamatella he lost track. And now she is putting such an emphasis on the word *tenth* that in all probability he will see her on Friday. Although the pleasure of anticipation begins immediately, it isn't without the disappointing awareness that the sole reason for her phone call is this business with the cemetery. Claire hates cemeteries and would never venture there on her own. He had liked her mother, and he is an obvious companion for this important anniversary. *The tyranny of round numbers,* thought Don. *And of basic biological functions demanding that I bring this conversation to an end before it's too late.*

"I will come. Shall I pick you up?" The Jewish cemetery is in Queens, and this is a legitimate offer.

"Oh, thank you. That would be lovely." He can hear her taking a breath before the "oh." The "lovely" is yet another of her favorite Briticisms.

"But you don't know where I live. Do you?" Of course he doesn't know, and this roundabout questioning is taking too much time.

"Give me the address. And your phone number as well, just in case something comes up." *Like thirty years ago,* he thought, *when I wanted so much to get her phone number. Time flies indeed.* It takes him ages to find a pen and there is no paper around, so he writes it all down on a one-pound bag of granulated sugar, the sharp nib piercing the bag in two places, white sugar escaping the confined space in great bursts, Claire insisting he repeat the information back to her. Then mission accomplished, a hasty goodbye, and finally, the bathroom.

✶✶✶✶✶

It is Friday afternoon, and they are sitting in a diner in Queens. The place is shabby and dark, and almost empty. The layout is classic: cubicles good for four people on one side, and cubicles for two on the other side. There are no chairs, and the vinyl-covered booths are dark red, very soft, and the places where they have been ripped open are covered with black tape. The place has known better days, but it is close to the cemetery, and there is no shortage of parking, making it an obvious stop after the brief visit to Claire's mother's grave. Facing each other, it is Don's first chance to have a close look at Claire. Earlier, while he was driving, any attempt to do that would have been too obvious, and if there is one thing that he wishes to avoid at all costs, it is doing or saying something that could appear too obvious. Or, for that matter, even too familiar. True, they are still officially married, but for all practical purposes they don't know each other. At least as far as he is concerned, he views himself as a different person. Well, even if not entirely different, still sufficiently so to prescribe a distance that precludes familiarity.

Even though the diner is far from being "a clean, well-lighted place"—*good old Hemingway lifting his head again,* he thought—it can't hide her beauty. The deeply set dark eyes are focused on his, and he feels himself melting under their spell. He notices that she has pulled her hair tightly back, leaving her ears and the tiny pearls that he had given her many years ago well exposed, tied in a classic bun on the back of her head. Of all the ways she does her hair he used to like this one best, and he still did. It certainly emphasizes her high cheekbones. Don is glad to see that like him, she has also obviously prepared herself for their meeting and wants to please him.

On their way to Queens they both felt awkward and talked mainly about the bad traffic, the oppressive heat, Naomi's decision to stay at school for the entire summer, David's apparent success at work, and how unbelievably fast the ten years since Claire's mother's death have gone by. *Like total strangers,* he thought, and dreaded the emptiness of the return trip. Claire is an only child, and he said the prayer for the dead. The ancient Aramaic text always gives him the creeps, but this time he liked the theatrical part of it. Then they both searched for a small stone to put on the grave and silently navigated the overcrowded cemetery. Near the exit several poor people demanded the traditional good deed, and he was more generous than usually, gratified to see that she noticed. It was then that she said that she was famished, and so here they are.

When the waiter, who looks as old as the establishment itself, comes to take their orders, Claire isn't ready yet, although she has been studying the menu for some time. Then, under pressure, she chooses a small Greek salad, without olive oil. The ancient waiter takes it down calmly, no doubt wondering what things have come to. Don feels a need to correct the impression and orders a pastrami sandwich with beer.

"I didn't know you like beer," she says.

"I have learned to like it. In Africa, coming back from a long day out in the bush, there is nothing like cold beer."

"You seem to have had a great time there."

"The best ever," he says, and realizing the implied accusation he quickly adds, "and I needed it." Another accusation. "It did me a lot of good." That was better. "I should have done it long ago." Much better, although he doesn't believe that he could ever have left for Africa before Claire left him. To be able to do that he would have needed to be in Africa first, but then that was *reduction ad absurdum.* He isn't sure if that is the correct Latin expression to describe a logical mess of this type, but this is hardly the time to think about it.

"How was the weather there?"

"Very mild. Much better than here. Most of Zimbabwe is a high plateau, so it never gets very hot or humid."

"And how about the roads? Do they have decent roads? And the hygiene, and all those diseases that one hears about?" Don can almost hear her adding, "that you used to talk about every time I suggested we go to some exotic place," but she controls herself, and if it is an attack, than it certainly isn't a direct one. His beer has just arrived, and he takes advantage of the time-out provided by the act of slowly filling the glass.

"Things are never as bad as the mass media makes them appear. The only major health problem there is AIDS, but that seems to be the case everywhere." Having said it, he can feel the sweet tension of having a secret that is his to share or withhold. There are many things he wants to share, things that are bursting from their protective hiding place dying to be told, and not just to anyone, but to this particular woman, but his AIDS secret isn't one of them. He can't understand what made him add that "their AIDS clinics are actually quite modern." This is provoking fate just a little too much, but with the help of the arrival of the small Greek salad that isn't small at all, it passes safely by without remark.

"Please don't wait, you must be very hungry."

"It's alright. I can wait." This with her famous hint of a smile, La Gioconda style. Don tries to communicate with the ancient waiter, but he is nowhere to be seen. However, the beeping sound of the microwave indicates that the pastrami is ready. Claire is surprised to see him picking up the thick sandwich from the plate and opening his mouth wide enough to manage a bite. Never in their life together has she seen him eat like this. He is always very meticulous about eating properly, cutting the food, any food, even a pastrami sandwich, into small pieces, and then expertly using his fork to lift them from the plate one at a time. But his hands? Never. She can't take her eyes off his fingers, now slightly glistening from the dripping fat, pressing into the rye bread. There is something exciting about it, full of vitality. First the beer, and now the sandwich…she feels confused. Their eyes meet, and for the first time since that fateful morning in the coffee shop near his office, he smiles his good broad smile at her.

"It's good to see you," she says.

"Same here," he says, struggling with the urge to add that he misses her. He knows that it will be a big mistake to say it, making her defensive, but it could also be a pleasant moment, and the temptation persists, so he asks her about her work instead. She takes a deep breath and speaks very softly, giving her voice the trembling touch that he likes so much.

"Oh, there's not a whole lot to say. I just want to make sure that each day I see some people, and do something productive. Besides, I like word processing, it's kind of fun. Actually, I go to the office only for a few hours, so that I still have time for other things."

Don hears the invitation, and stopping halfway through pouring himself some more beer, he dutifully asks about the other things. Then he hears about the gym, and about the diet, and about "Modern Life and Total Health," and how both Marion and Claire take this course very seriously and read a great deal of interesting articles, and about the lecture series at the Frick Collection, and about the opera, and finally about the forthcoming trip to Paris. There is something desperate about all of this, and Don can see the two women jogging from one event to another to make the most of what a day can offer. He is more impressed by what she doesn't mention than by what she does, but he realizes that this might only be the first, partial list. If he had to make a quick list of his experiences in Africa, that would also be misleading.

"But Paris is nothing compared with your adventures. You must tell me about the trip. I absolutely insist." *Another British expression,* thought Don, wishing that she wouldn't use them so often. However, the "insist" leaves little room for debate, and he finds himself talking about the Falls, and about the strong African light, the evening fires, the incredible beauty of the stars, and before he can do anything about it he is describing the morning walk from Robins Camp, when the cheeky lioness charged the small group of tourists.

In the middle of the story he orders a cup of decaffeinated coffee for Claire, and another beer for himself. He "insists" on details, although they are selected with care. The search for the pugmarks of the lion, the elaborate tracking with him being chosen as the "tailing Charlie," Lucky's rifle at the ready, the oppressive heat, the need for absolute silence, and then the sight of the sleek and impressive beast. He spoke with great gusto, changing tempo, using a wide range of tones. Having wiped his fingers on the napkin, he uses both hands for emphasis. It is clear that the story is having a great effect on Claire, and he doesn't want to finish it. He can sense her excitement when the lioness finally attacked, and rounds it off with the phrase, "It was a perfect moment to die," thinking to himself that if it worked once, it may work again.

Now that it is over, Don's elation subsides quickly. The way he tells this story, though a good one, is after all basically false. Without the lovemaking part, both the lions' and his own, it doesn't amount to much. It is just an empty shell, or better still, a shell that if cracked will uncover something rotten, like the walnuts. So, should he tell her about Iris? For a brief moment he is tempted, but even while the temptation is at its strongest he knows that he won't do it. Iris is out and at least for the time being so is anything personal. For all he knows, this estranged wife of his, in spite of showing keen interest in him, in spite of "absolutely insisting" on listening to his adventures, might be living with the lover for whom she left him in the first place. Otherwise it doesn't make any sense. Would she leave him just to have more time to spend with her health nut of a friend running between the gym and some guru lecturing about the wisdom of the East? She could have done that without breaking up their marriage! Easily! *Eas-ily!* The old anger is now coming back in full force, and he has to do something about it.

"I hope to leave everything and go back there soon." Don isn't so sure that this will happen, certainly not after his initial search for a potential buyer for his company. He isn't even sure anymore whether he wants to do it, since that impulsive idea forced itself into his mind he has had a lot of time to weigh the pros and cons of such a major move. Right now, however, all he wants is to say something outrageous, something that will shock her and perhaps even hurt.

"Another trip? So soon?"

"No, this time it will be for good."

"You can't be serious. Are you?" Even as she says it Claire knows that he is serious. Don is always serious; that is one of his main problems.

"I am serious. There's nothing that can keep me here." He wants to emphasize the "nothing," since he considers himself a sort of expert on nothingness, but there is no need to overdo it.

"What about your company? Your work?"

Fuck the company, fuck the work, thought Don. Where were they in his hour of need? And besides, he is not some kind of a workaholic, not anymore. True, recently he has been more energetic in the mornings, and once or twice he has even looked forward to his work, but that doesn't make him a slave yet. He is free to come and go as he wishes. Almost free. Almost like Mwewe. He leans close to her as if to share a secret, and tells her, "There is more to life than work, and there are mysteries that I still hope to unravel, and in any event, I have embarked on a road from which there is no turning back."

Don realizes that the situation is becoming a little dramatic. He worries that he may have committed himself to something that he might be sorry about later, but the unfolding spectacle is too intoxicating. He feels a mixture of power and lightness, but now that he has played his winning card there is nothing more he can do to press his advantage. At least not right away, so he just sits there waiting to see what happens next. Claire seems confused and doesn't know how to react. That much he can see in her eyes, which are looking at him in bewilderment. She takes another sip of coffee, although he suspects that the mug is empty. It's something he would do in a situation like this, but seeing her in his place is a new experience. Now is the perfect time to say goodbye, a perfect exit. That, however, isn't in the cards, and they will have to remain together for the entire drive back, in the confined space of his car. A perfect anticlimax, that's what's in store for them.

And so it is, in spite of several attempts by Claire to stimulate the conversation. It takes them almost half an hour to reach the tunnel, and throughout that largely uneventful time she does her best to sound cheerful. This is accompanied by great—he thinks exaggerated—movement of her entire upper body so that she almost faces him. On his part, Don wants to maintain some form of serious detachment and barely responds. There is some pleasure in watching her try so hard to rouse his interest, and when she says that she hopes to see him again soon just as she was about to get out of the car, he is flattered and sufficiently mollified to discard his newly discovered sulking role and express his hope for the same.

"Let's have dinner sometime soon," she says.

"I would love that very much."

"Should I call you to set something up?"

"Please do," says Don, and the happiness that sweeps over him without any warning is so sudden that without hesitation he adds, "I've missed you." It's as if the words have been there all this time waiting for the first opportunity to squeeze past his self-control.

"I've missed you too," she says, and leaving her wide smile behind, she went into her building.

Despite having already left her three messages saying to call back immediately, Claire keeps trying Marion's number. When she finally calls back she can't wait to tell her about her impressions.

"Where have you been? I've been desperate to talk to you."

"I know, I just now saw all your messages."

"What took you so long to get back to me?"

"Come on, Claire, don't be ridiculous. I called you right away."

"Alright, alright."

"Do I sense impatience? You have something to tell me. How did it go today?"

"I don't know, actually. It was so strange, so unlike anything I could have expected that I'm all mixed up."

"Did you enjoy it?"

"Enjoyment is not the issue. We went to the cemetery first, and then stopped for a bite at a diner. The thing that fascinated me is that

Don acted very different than before. It's not that people can't change, but look, I've known him for more than twenty years now, I mean *really* known him. There are no surprises anymore. I knew exactly what he'd do, what he'd say, when, and how he'd phrase it. You know that was the thing I hated most, this total predictability. It was so boooring."

"Yeah?"

"Well, today he surprised me constantly. I'm serious, Marion, it was as if I didn't know him at all."

"Could you give me an example?"

"Sure. Plenty of examples. It started with the beer. No, actually it started in the cemetery. There was a sort of serenity about him that I didn't recognize. And he was so generous with the alms, I mean, *really* generous. But let me tell you about the beer. Don is a water person. Occasionally he'll have a Coke or a Sprite, but never a beer. He used to consider it too vulgar. Well, he had two of them today, and he ate his pastrami sandwich with his bare hands."

"Sounds like a macho man to me."

"Well, you could put it that way, but for me it was a revelation. But it was the way he talked that I found the strangest. You should've seen his excitement, and he was talkative. It was such a beautiful sight."

"Do you mean to tell me that he turned you on?"

"Don't be such a bitch, Marion. You know what I mean."

"Do I? It seems to me that your ex-husband is about to reconquer his territory."

Claire, aware of Marion's jealousy, didn't want to push the point too far. To satisfy her, she said, "I wonder if there isn't another woman. Sometimes you can feel these things. Perhaps she's waiting for him in Africa, and that's why he plans to return there."

"Don? Another woman? No way, you must be crazy."

"I don't know. You'd think a woman would be capable of transforming a man like that."

"And what is this thing about returning to Africa?"

"He plans to return there for good. He said there's more to life than work, and something about magic, and—wait a minute, it wasn't magic, but something similar—and that there was nothing to keep him here."

"You can't possibly let him go without getting a proper divorce first. It's too risky. He might get lost somewhere in the jungle and you'd be stuck here. And then there are financial considerations, of course. I really think you shouldn't delay this any longer."

"Marion, please don't get carried away. I can take care of myself. It isn't like he's leaving tomorrow. At least I don't think he is. Besides, I'm not so sure I want to rush the formalities. I have to think about it. There are many things I have to think about."

For some reason Claire doesn't feel free to tell her best friend about her upcoming dinner plans with Don. She suspects objections of all sorts, some of them probably justified, but she doesn't want to hear them. Perhaps later.

Window

"Let's try a few more," Irv says as he switches on the tape recorder. It took him some time to realize that without recording their sessions they lost precious material. Don's reactions to acronymic stimulation are so fast that Irv can't possibly keep up. "Tell me when you're ready."

"I'm ready," said Don.

"TIME."

"Travel In Middle Experience."

"What do you mean by that?"

"Life, I mean, life itself is travel in middle experience. At first, when you're young, there is only the future, and the next thing you know there is only the past. Life itself is somewhere in the middle, but time travels so fast that there is very little of it."

"IRV."

"Intimacy Requires Valor."

"Well, well. Let's see what we have here. Are you afraid of intimacy?"

"Isn't everybody?"

"Perhaps, to some degree. In your case, however, there could be some extra need to protect yourself from intimacy. Can you think of something related to this?"

"Sure. Take Iris. My impotence wasn't a chance event—it served its purpose. And then when I overcame that hurdle I got myself all worked up with my crazy worries about AIDS, which made absolutely certain that not a shred of intimacy could survive. Or take logovory. Isn't that also an attempt to keep myself from getting intimate with the meanings of words? Intimate may not be the right word for it, but its purpose seems to be to keep my distance from them."

"Yes. Very good. Very good indeed."

His patient has made so much progress lately that Irv is willing to take him through the next step. It is an intellectual gamble, he knows, but one worth trying. For years he has been struggling with some innovative ideas that can only be tested with a few special patients. When Don first came to him, he considered him to be the last person on earth with whom he could try it, but not anymore. The African trip has given him enough raw materials to work with, and now that this acronymy has come up, it makes sense to try.

"Do you remember when you told me your African friend's story?"

"Mwewe? Sure, I remember everything."

"Do you remember the part just before the shooting when he wasn't sure which road to take and then took one without knowing what would happen next?"

"Yes. What about it?"

"Can you put yourself in his place? I mean, can you actually experience that particular moment?"

"I can try, though it isn't easy."

"How do you go about trying?"

"I concentrate on the details of what he told me and attempt to put myself in his place."

"Good. Do it now."

Don closes his eyes and goes about his mission. First he evokes the memory of Mwewe's face, the way he had sat across from him at the bar. The eyes and the hair are OK, but the rest of the face is fuzzy. Next he tries to see the small gully that provides reasonable cover, but it's too rocky, and walking there will make a lot of noise. The road straight ahead, though softer, is more exposed. He recalls that on a night like this sounds carry farther than eyes can see, and he is tempted to go straight ahead. But something doesn't feel right. He is confused, he can't make up his mind, and then he takes the company straight ahead. Still, he can't feel it. The moment is alright, but it isn't his moment, and he doesn't know how to feel it. Frustrated, he opens his eyes.

"How did it go?"

"Not so well. I think I know what someone in this situation should feel, but without actually being there, it's too theoretical."

"Would you like me to help you?"

"Of course."

"Can you think of something that happened to you that even though very different, might have produced a similar state of mind?"

"I'm not sure I understand."

"Let's assume that Mwewe's experience produced great tension, and even though it's not under his control, there's hope that things will turn out alright. What I'm suggesting is that you might have been through an entirely different experience that nevertheless evoked very similar feelings."

"I see. Yes, I can think of two such experiences off the top of my head. The first was the moment when the bull elephant approached the car from behind, and all I could do was hope he would spare me."

"And the second?"

"In the AIDS clinic, when I went into the office to hear the results. It could have gone either way. Now that I think of it, although the two events are different, they produced very similar feelings."

"Excellent! You really are extremely good at this."

Don is glad to hear the compliment, particularly since Irv's excitement is so evident. He still has no idea what the purpose of all this is though.

"How about a milder version of the same state of mind? Can you think of something less important, almost mundane, that gave you the feeling that anything could happen in the next moment?"

Don takes his time. Whereas the previous examples presented themselves almost automatically, the task of looking for unimportant events seems much more difficult. There are only a few dramatic events that come to mind, but countless mundane ones, so how should he go about searching for something that abstract? After a long pause, he manages to come up with a good example. "Opening a mailbox. Or, better yet, opening a letter from someone that you can't immediately recognize. I recall the feeling I had when I got the letter from Iris. The type of excitement I felt before finding out who had sent it was, I think, similar to that produced by the other examples, although much less extreme, of course." And as an afterthought, he adds, "Now that I think of it, something like this happened the other day when I received this unexpected phone call. As a matter of fact, to some degree it happens every time the phone rings, since just before finding out who's calling, anything is possible."

Irv is glad that the entire session is being recorded, since nobody that he has introduced to his notion about states of mind has picked it up as quickly and as effectively as Don. He is confident that it is the one thing that can do his patient a lot of good. On top of that, he needs this type of material for his upcoming lecture in which he intends to introduce his ideas to the public for the first time.

"Do you want to try now once again to put yourself in Mwewe's position?"

"Yes, but how should I go about it this time?"

"Instead of trying to evoke a feeling that you expect him to have felt, let the events that you yourself experienced get you there. It doesn't even matter which one you choose—in principle they are all interchangeable."

And so Don finds himself once more contemplating the two roads ahead of him, and he can't make up his mind, and then he chooses the one ahead, and as he does it he feels the tension in the AIDS clinic, hoping that the verdict is in his favor. It works. The two situations blend together, and he is excited to realize that he can feel something that he has never experienced before. There are so many things that he hasn't experienced himself that the possibility of being in possession of a key to their secrets is very exciting.

"I don't believe this. Where did you learn this trick?"

"There is no trick," says Irv, obviously pleased with the success of his demonstration. "It is a skill that has the potential to liberate us from our own limited experience, and it can be cultivated. What you need more than anything is a lot of practice. And a lot of practice you shall have."

"I still can't get over it. Why didn't you tell me about it before? I could have made good use of it."

"No, you couldn't. But now, perhaps, you can. So let me give you your first homework assignment concerning states of mind. You have been saying how much you miss Africa, and how much you would like to go back there. Well, your task is to pay attention to anything happening here that evokes in you some of the states of mind that you experienced in Africa. Each time you recognize one, make sure to get it down in writing. Would you like to do that?"

"I can try, and we'll see what happens."

"Good. However, let me caution you not to attempt anything deliberate. You can't wish a state of mind into existence, nor can you chase after one—it must come to you."

Jordan (Mwewe) Mpulia, M.Sc.
Geologist
Ganzell Mining Company
Total House
Bulawayo, Zimbabwe

New York, July 9

My dear Mwewe,

It is now almost ten in the evening and there is still some light outside. Very different from your country. There is nothing I would like to do more right now than drive somewhere between Hwange and Bulawayo, with the road almost entirely empty, and with plenty of time to observe and think. I would arrive at your place unannounced just like you came to see me, and I would ask you to take me to your Matopos. Yes, that's what I would enjoy most, but it doesn't seem that I'll be able to do this soon. There are too many things to be done here, and when some of them are done new tasks take their place. I found a potential buyer for my shares in the company, but I'm not sure that I want to sell, and recently even my wife is courting my friendship. As you can see, I have indeed embarked on a journey from which there is no coming back. The road isn't easy, but it's a good road, worthy of the effort.

My dear man of mystery, you should know that you have become an important part of my life, and I'm thankful for that. I often think of you and of the wonderful time I spent in Africa. The thoughts come to me in many ways. Here are a few examples:

This morning, in my office, I used a small ladder to reach the top shelf of the bookcase, and suddenly, looking down from above,

I felt like a giraffe. You may think that I'm exaggerating, but believe me that I didn't invent this sensation, nor did I chase after it—quite the contrary, the realization that this is how a giraffe must feel came to me on its own. Standing there, for a brief moment I could actually sense the flexibility of my neck, as if it were much longer. The whole thing took only a few seconds, but it gave me great pleasure. I still remember the last giraffe I watched on my last day in Sinamatella, and how it disappeared into the acacia forest. You see, I have been using that ladder for years and years, but it has never been anything but a pragmatic tool to reach a particular volume of regulations published by the IRS. This morning, however, it was entirely different. The simple act had gained enormous value.

Did you know that a traffic light in the big city is like a water hole? Here's why. A few days ago, during my lunch break, I went for a walk. The weather was hot and I walked very slowly as if I had all the time in the world. The way elephants walk. All around me people were scurrying in all directions, and I alone was unperturbed, trudging ahead, my steps well measured and yet with that added bounce of lightness to them that's so wonderful to watch. I saw the traffic light ahead of me, its "WALK" command clearly visible. Then the light started to flash, indicatingthat it was about to change soon. I didn't want to stop moving and wait, so I quickened my stride to cross the street in time. It was almost automatic, the way elephants speed up briefly when approaching a water hole. So here you have it, a water hole and a traffic light. Again, for a moment the two were interchangeable. More important, however, since that afternoon I have enjoyed walking the busy streets of New York more than ever before.

Speaking of elephants, I have just been reading *The Roots of Heaven* by Romain Gary, which is about a quixotic attempt to save them from extinction. The hero of the book was held in a Nazi concentration camp, and every time he was on the verge of collapse he tried to imagine a long line of elephants walking freely across the landscape. It was this particular image, the picture of ultimate freedom, that saved him from total despair. When he survived, he thought that he owed the elephants his protection. I liked the story and was sorry to learn that the author died some years ago. It would have been good to know a person like him, for he too must have been a man of mystery.

Do you know how I define a man of mystery lately? He is someone who knows things without having experienced them before. He can sense things from other things, like when you are searching for water, or when you were scouting during the war. I'm finding that situations share many properties and produce similar states of mind. Consequently, if one is alert enough and open to experience, one can know one thing from knowing another. Does that make sense to you?

I have a confession to make, and since it concerns you in a way, I would rather make it to you than to anybody else. Ever since I heard your story I have found myself fascinated by the limits of rationality, and the need to be open to one's intuitions. You see, Mwewe, this may be obvious to you, but I was trained in a very different tradition. For me anything that is beyond the rational and the scientific is first and foremost irrational. As such it has no place in any serious consideration. In fact, all of civilization can be seen as an attempt to suppress irrationality and pave the way for scientific enlightenment. Your worldview allows for the presence of mystery side by side with science and technology, and I have learned to appreciate its richness. One step at a time, I have become fascinated by the slightest suggestion of the presence of mystery, and the minutest coincidence has become an opportunity for celebrating my newly discovered rebellion. You may consider my attempts to bring the elephants and the giraffes into my city life as yet another example of this tendency, although in this case I was instructed to do this by my therapist.

This brings me to my confession. You see, even in the mist of it all, I have my doubts. I look at myself from some distance, and I keep wondering: Am I trying too hard to believe in something that is basically not true? Am I working myself into some artificial excitement for nothing? Did you notice that *DON* can stand for *Drunk On Nothingness*? Yes, my friend, I'm open to new experience; I would even go with you to Matopos, but at the same time a small part of me keeps watching with skepticism bordering on the cynical. And even though I want to get rid of that part of myself, it just won't go. I hope this doesn't disappoint you too much. I hope you understand that your friend from New York wasn't reborn in Sinamatella; he was at best given a helpful nudge to slightly change course.

You may have been right in telling me that there is no way back, but one can certainly look over one's shoulder, don't you think? There is an absurd, almost perverse pleasure in honestly realizing the limits of one's vision.

Stay well, Mwewe. I miss you.

Don

Meaning

"Ladies and gentlemen, our speaker today doesn't need an introduction in this forum. We have had the pleasure of listening to Dr. Irving Hunt on several occasions before. His ideas are always fascinating and provoke heated discussions. I am confident that this will also hold true today. The title of his talk is "Microlife vs. Macrolife". Dr. Hunt, please, the floor is yours."

The room is packed, and Irv is gratified to see quite a few professional authorities in the audience. He knows that he has something quite extraordinary to tell them and has been looking forward to this opportunity for some time already. Opposition to his ideas is inevitable, particularly from the traditional establishment.

Some of the more progressive members with a humanistic psychology orientation with whom he felt close affinity will also be bothered by what they will see as an attack on classic logotherapy. *It will be interesting,* he thought to himself as he approached the head of the table, nodding his thanks to the perfunctory applause. He prefers to remain standing, something that always enhances the quality of his delivery. At first he plans to open with a joke to parry any anticipatory antagonism that may be lurking in the room, but after some thought he decides against it, opting for the standard approach instead. For the same reason he has prepared his presentation in writing, although he will in all likelihood improvise whenever possible.

"Thank you, Mr. Chairman, for your kind words; I will do my best not to disappoint you. Ladies and gentlemen, I feel privileged to have the opportunity to share with you some new ideas and am looking forward to the discussion segment of this meeting. Before we reach that point, I hope to present some theoretical notions, as well as a clinical case that demonstrates the main issues.

"With your permission, let me start by saying a few words about the title itself. *Macrolife* refers to involvement in events taking place in the external world. We live macrolife when we interact with reality. This is in contrast to *microlife*, which refers to the internal life of the mind. Needless to say, microlife often reflects things that have happened or that we wish would happen in macrolife. Consequently, internal reality is in some respect reactive to what external reality has to offer.

"Question: Can fantasy life, even a very rich fantasy life, compete with the real thing?

"Question: To what extent is it possible to have a rich fantasy life in a highly routine and uneventful environment?

"Question: When does a rich fantasy life become a major obstacle to effective reality orientation? Is psychosis the ultimate model for the dangers of microlife in its extreme?

"Question: Does a life of adventure necessarily limit the richness of internal life? Or, stated differently, can an extrovert enjoy the pleasures of introversion?

"The questions are many, and I could go on like this for the entire time that you have kindly allocated for my lecture. Instead, let me simply point out that in our clinical practices we often come across patients with an obvious imbalance between macro and microlife. I venture to add that with the rare exception of psychopaths, the imbalance leans heavily toward the internal. Many of our patients feel that their lives are boring, uneventful, and devoid of meaning. In this they are by no means exceptional; the basic existential crisis can certainly be found well beyond the domain of psychopathology. The problem is that no amount of compensatory fantasy can hide the fact that nothing is happening, and that which happens if often meaningless.

"Some compensatory mechanisms may actually backfire. Take for instance television, certainly a leading compensatory device. So much is happening on the small screen so quickly that in contrast, one's own life appears to be even drearier than before. No amount of vicarious macrolife can infuse drama into the private lives of passive spectators.

"These problems are exacerbated further when a person has neither microlife nor macrolife, but carries on like an empty automaton. The causes for the emergence of this condition vary, but once established it is extremely resistant to change. Sometimes the only opportunity to overcome such total malaise presents itself in the form of a major trauma. That brings us to the clinical case study that will be our focus today.

"D. is a man of fifty-two, married but separated, father of two children who live away from home, working as a successful accountant. He came to see me six months ago, shortly after his wife left him. When he arrived he was severely depressed and plagued by recurring suicidal thoughts. According to him the sudden split with his wife came as a total surprise. He loved his wife dearly and was confident that everything was fine between them. Shattered by her departure, he felt that he had nothing left and nobody to turn to for support. All his friends were couples who were recruited and cultivated by his wife; he had no close friends of his own. His relationships with both of his children were superficial and distant, and he found himself entirely alone.

"Even a brief interaction with D. sufficed to expose his obsessive-compulsive character. Everything he did was completely routine and stylized. The same applied to his thoughts, so that following the traumatic abandonment by his wife they became a major source of torment. For hours on end he tortured himself with visions of her and her presumed lover, whose existence he needed to account for her decision to leave him. It turned out, however, that many years ago he had developed certain obsessions that effectively prevented him from thinking. A leading obsession of his consisted of taking a word and searching for its exact center. The routine for this prescribed that he first count the number of letters, which was typically done by breaking them into groups of two or three. If the result was an odd number, the midpoint became the remaining letter. If it was an even number, the midpoint was between two letters. He would then spell the word in a particular fashion, emphasizing the solution to the problem. In his mind, this breaking of words into their constituent fragments was called *logovory.* So frequent was this logovory that it prevented him from spending any significant time thinking about the meanings of words; they became simply the targets for his obsession. Over the course of several sessions it was revealed that whenever a word or a phrase triggered a train of thought that was threatening, he would quickly cut off the stream of associations and search for the center of a particularly long word instead. It was a perfect way to neutralize potentially painful thoughts. Since logovory required his full attention, it acted as a potent disinfectant.

"At this point, ladies and gentlemen, you may undoubtedly wonder about its symbolic meaning. On this account D. himself volunteered several impressive insights. Two of them warrant a brief mention. First, he thought that searching for the midpoint of a word related to his need for symmetry and order as opposed to chaos. He abhorred anything chaotic and unpredictable. All his life, he said, was an attempt to tame the turmoil that he sensed pervaded everything, himself included, and impose on it some structure. Second, and probably more important, D. was clearly anxious about old age and death. He realized that the midpoint of his life was long past, and that what remained in store for him was the permanent decline toward death. 'Dwelling on nothingness,' he called it. This existential crisis preceded the trauma, but its realization came only later. The paradox was that his success at routinizing his life left him with nothing to look forward to. Thus, as if often the case, the two factors behind his obsession were in direct conflict with each other.

"Stated differently, the anticipated absence of macrolife was so threatening to him that he stifled any attempt to develop microlife instead. Although a highly intelligent and caring person, he became entirely predictable, and boring. That, according to his wife's testimony, was the main reason for her decision to leave him. Much to his credit, after the initial crisis was over, he also admitted that this extreme sterility of his must have turned her off. That, however, only came later. Shortly after his wife left him without any advance warning, he found himself in the center of a totally chaotic experience, with little or no insight into his condition.

"During one of our early sessions I asked him to tell me something exciting that had happened to him, but he was unable to come up with anything at all. At that point he had to admit that his wife leaving was the only dramatic event in his entire life. As such, it presented a potential opportunity for change. The main question, of course, is: Change to what? Is there something worthwhile that we, in this helpful profession, can offer a person who is in a deep existential crisis? Sure, we can and should offer competent first aid to an individual in reactive depression with a clear, trauma-related onset. But what can we offer beyond first aid? Don't most people deny death in order to maintain a sufficiently high morale as a prerequisite to proper functioning? Do we consider such self-deception indicative of a strong ego, or rather an infantile attempt against reality testing? Isn't, in fact, the honest realization of one's mortality an indication of maturity and health?

"It is at this point that those of you with inclinations toward logotherapy may feel that in contrast to other types of treatments you have something important to offer. Isn't the existential condition a symptom of a life devoid of meaning? What else but a successful quest for meaning could rekindle one's spirit and regenerate the vitality that has gone? Unfortunately I do not share such optimism, and can't embrace it as a therapeutic guideline. I will gladly develop this theme further, if you would like, during the discussion segment. Right now let me just say that before taking that route, I would have to be convinced that there is a reasonable chance that the patient's search for meaning will, in fact, yield something of value.

"Let me propose that there is, however, another way that is directly related to our central topic today. It consists of enriching one's mundane experiences through a procedure I call *states of mind*. Effective utilization of states of mind allows us to enjoy some important aspects of macrolife within the more confined context of microlife. With your permission, let me try to introduce this idea in a more systematic manner.

"Many entirely different events share identical or extremely similar states of mind. An illustration might be helpful. Consider the situation of a person tried for some serious offense who is just about to hear the verdict. We believe that we can to some extent know that person's experience via identification and empathy. But none of these worthy concepts gets down to the bottom of the issue: Is it possible to truly know something without having experienced it before? From the vantage point of my argument the answer is clearly yes, since despite never having been in the precise circumstances of that other person, we have on many occasions experienced the same state of mind. Thus each time we open our mailbox or a letter from somebody that we don't recognize, for a brief moment we wait for the verdict. The amount of tension is, of course, different, but the feeling is the same. In fact, whenever we pick up a ringing phone, we experience a brief moment of anticipation that shares some important elements with the case of the accused. The process we call empathy builds on actual experience with overlapping states of mind.

"The wisdom of language has recognized this long ago, as witnessed by the construction of metaphors. Watching the sun rise over the horizon produces the same state of mind as that of watching a birth, and the setting sun invariably evokes feelings of ending and death. In the same manner, crossing a bridge necessarily produces the state of mind as a commitment to a course of action.

"I wish to propose that different types of experience far outnumber the different types of states of mind. Consequently, many different experiences share the same state of mind. This brings us to the issue of macrolife versus microlife. If I am indeed correct in my assumptions, it should follow that one could, in principle, have access to important aspects of macrolife within the context of a more limited microlife. We cannot expect everyone who is having an existential crisis to just leave everything and try to immerse him or herself in action. Fortunately the drama of adventure can to some extent be known and lived even within the confined existence of mundane and routine life. Knowing how to use states of mind can significantly enrich our quality of life.

"It is not an easy matter, and it requires both sensitivity and training. It also requires two additional things, neither of which D. possessed at the time: a measure of openness to experience, and sufficient raw material to work with. My first problem was to unfreeze a totally frozen personality. This, according to my limited experience, is best achieved by exposure to intense sensory stimulation. In short, after the initial crisis was over, I suggested a trip to Africa. With some obvious skepticism he agreed to take a guided tour to Zimbabwe, which turned out to be more effective than I had hoped. In fact, two weeks into the tour he decided to leave the group and stay on his own until he had a chance 'to sort things out.' Unfortunately, his stay was cut short due to an obsessive worry of his own creation, thus reminding us that D. is essentially a highly vulnerable person in need of help. At the same time, before his return home, there were several positive developments that should be briefly mentioned.

"First of all, on a few occasions he found himself at the center of high drama. There were two life-threatening situations, the second one occurring when he was alone. There's nothing like that to give a person a good shake and reorder his priorities. Such macro-experience also provides excellent raw material for what is to follow. He became friendly with an African who turned out to be an outstanding individual. This friend, who embodied a complex mixture of modernity and African tradition, played a major role in D.'s unfreezing. Specifically, it was his involvement with mysteries, intuitions, and coincidences that unhinged D. from his rigid preconceptions and prepared him for what was perhaps the most fascinating development of all, since it made use of his obsessive-compulsive tendencies to forge an effective weapon against them.

"Ladies and gentlemen, having told you about logovory, let me now tell you about *acronymy*. It consists of the urge to view words as acronyms, and, after separating them into their constituent letters, to search for the words that they stand for. Thus D. took my name, Irv, and came up with "Intimacy Requires Valor." Upon presented with a word like *day*, he immediately answered with "Day As Year" and proceeded to describe his fear that time was running out too fast. His capacity for this type of obsessive yet creative engagement was so great that for a while I used it as a tool for information gathering. When presented with a word, any word, his answer came so quickly that I suspected something akin to automatic writing, with direct access to unconscious material. The superficial affinity of acronymy to logovory is obvious. In both cases words are divided into letters. However, whereas in the former this was done as a preparation for counting the letters, in the latter it was the first stage toward creating new meanings. D. himself was often surprised by what came out, and he enjoyed the entire process. Needless to say, whereas logovory always produced the same solution, this was not the case here. On the contrary, the same word could be the stimulus for entirely different solutions. In short, D.'s latest obsession was a highly dynamic and creative one. As such, it indicated that he was now ready for the next phase of treatment.

"It was at this point that I introduced him to states of mind and proceeded to give him homework assignments for training. The initial steps in this type of mental activity are particularly difficult since the inexperienced cannot evoke it, nor can one chase after it. The best modus operandi appears to be one of passivity mixed with vigilance. The task during those first steps is to recognize a state of mind when it is one's own. At this stage one is continuously on the lookout for a state of mind that can take one beyond the present situation that evoked it. Someone who can make use of this idea is always on the verge of flying, perched on a rock, trying to catch the right wind. Only after long training can this 'art,' if I am allowed to call it that, be practiced purposefully.

"Our patient, D., though making good progress, is still not at that stage. He has managed to rid himself of some of his obsessions, but only to a limited degree. He has also succeeded in developing a more daring, risk-taking attitude toward life, but also only to a limited degree. His road to controlled usage of states of mind is still a long one. Once that point is reached, the enterprise becomes a deliberate attempt to enrich one's existence by the infusion of extra meaning. This requires a major effort, and must be carried out with the full awareness of what it stands for, and what it can accomplish. Its only purpose is to momentarily enrich the drabness of life, without any illusions as to its higher purpose. In a way, it is a compliment to oneself.

"Ladies and gentlemen, I have already taken much of your time, and I would now like to end this presentation with a quote from *The Myth of Sisyphus* by Albert Camus. He writes, 'I leave Sisyphus at the foot of the mountain! One always finds one's burden again. But Sisyphus teaches the higher fidelity that negates the gods and raises rocks. He too concludes that all is well. This universe henceforth without a master seems to him neither sterile nor futile. Each atom of that stone, each mineral flake of that night-filled mountain, in itself forms a world. The struggle itself toward the heights is enough to fill a man's heart. One must imagine Sisyphus happy.'"

The applause, though longer and louder than Irv had expected, doesn't fool him. He knows the enormous, almost mythical power of a good quote at the end of a lecture. It draws its strength, he thinks, from evoking a particularly receptive and appreciative state of mind. He knows that he has given a good lecture, and he felt the audience with him throughout the entire hour, but it is Albert Camus that is getting most of the applause, not his arguments. There is something almost awe inspiring in the last sentence that made him want to finish the whole thing right there, rather than break the impact as any question or comment from the floor inevitably must. His audience must feel the same, because for several long seconds nobody wishes to speak. He almost starts to delude himself into hoping that the shock of what he has said is powerful enough to leave them speechless, when the chairman thanks him for a most interesting lecture and invites the discussion to begin.

The spell broken, the first hand quickly raises in the front row. It belongs to one of the most distinguished members of the "old guard," a man with a traditional psychoanalytic orientation. The long silver hair and the hint of a German accent are classic, almost stereotypic. As he starts talking he keeps turning his head toward the rest of the audience, and it is obvious that he isn't addressing his remarks to the speaker, but rather to the public at large. Irv knows this man and doesn't expect anything original from him, but he is in for a big surprise.

"My point is not directly related to the main topic of this lecture, but it is a very important one. I want to go beyond what you, Dr. Hunt, told us about states of mind, and explore whether this concept can help us resolve an old theoretical debate that has been going on in the psychoanalytic community almost since the days of its origins in Vienna. I particularly liked the way you illustrated what you meant by these states of mind. You used the examples of sunrise, sunset, and crossing a bridge. If what you said is correct, it would make these events into universal symbols of birth, or death, or commitment. But if your theory of states of mind can explain the existence of universal symbols, it has a direct impact on Jung's claim for the so-called 'collective unconscious.' I am sure that some of my Jungian colleagues would not like this, but once again we have proof that universal symbols, and perhaps universal myths and stories as well, need not be based on such mystical notions as were suggested by Jung. You must have thought about this, I'm sure, and I would be glad to hear your comments."

The truth is that Irv has never thought about this excellent point before, and he quickly says so. Admitting ignorance is, he knows, almost as good as quoting Camus.

The next commentator, also from the old guard, points out that logovory implies the swallowing, perhaps devouring of words, and might suggest that D. feels empty inside and needs to fill himself with anything available. This is more in the classic tradition, and Irv agrees that it is possible, and that such interpretation will only reinforce the feeling of his patient's "nothingness," and that on one occasion D. had talked about the affinity between his "word processing" and "food processing" and Irv ends his response by saying that there is some food for thought in all of this.

Time is running out, and the chairman invites the last two comments. The first, from a very young man sitting next to one of the massive pillars toward the end of the hall who has to raise his voice to be heard, inquires whether Dr. Hunt has thought that states of mind are useful only in therapy, or whether they could be as effective, in fact perhaps even more effective, in the service of healthy individuals? Irv could have killed himself for forgetting to mention this during his main talk and thanks the commentator for providing him the opportunity to do so now: "The potential enrichment of mundane life is, of course, relevant to most of us. In the case of some patients with acute existential crisis, the need is more obvious, but yes, it definitely transcends psychotherapy, and should be viewed as a universal approach, at least in the developed, post-modern societies."

The last question comes from a middle-aged woman in front who clearly disagreed with him several times during the lecture. Her body language had left nothing to the imagination. She almost stood up waving her hand, anxiously demanding to be recognized by the chairman. Now that she has been given the floor she is very excited and throughout her comment remains in the awkward position halfway between sitting and standing. But hers is the question that he has been waiting for. It concerns the difference between logotherapy and states of mind. The difference between the search for meaning and the infusion of meaning. He is glad that it has finally arrived.

"The difference between the two cannot be overstated. Whereas logotherapy assumes that lives, all lives, have meaning that can be discovered, my starting assumption is that this is not necessarily the case. In the absence of religious belief, or when, as Nietzsche put it, 'God is dead,' the meaning of life cannot be taken for granted. Even a major effort to search for meaning can come up short, leaving the individual more frustrated than before the attempt. And yet, in the best of the existential tradition, it's possible to be aware of the fact that life is meaningless, and at the same time try to do something with it. For what could be more futile than the fate of Sisyphus himself? Were he to develop chronic depression it would be the most logical outcome of his situation. Instead, as Camus points out, he decides that in spite of everything he will try to infuse into his miserable ordeal some meaning in order to lighten his burden. However, such a noble effort deserves our admiration only on the condition that it does not cultivate an illusion. Sisyphus becomes a hero to the extent that he recognizes his attempts to infuse meaning in his life exactly for what they are.

"In the same way, D., or for that matter anybody trying to invest some effort in the enrichment of everyday life, should be aware that the basic tenets of the human condition are not changed by any of this. A cosmetic treatment at best, but in the absence of other options, it is all there is. No illusions, please, no denial, no 'willing suspension of disbelief,' not even a short one.

"To the extent that one is able to make good use of the richness that states of mind have to offer, one embarks on a great adventure. That, however, is not a single grand discovery that gives meaning to everything that follows, but rather a day-to-day, moment-to-moment struggle. Thank you."

Epilogue

In his office, fondling the clean, laser-printed sheets of his latest report, he likes the touch of the finished product, since it is a tangible expression of his work. Several days ago he insisted on upgrading the quality of the paper they use for reports, and he can now feel how much heavier it is than the stuff they had been using for years. *Don counts the pages once more. He knows that there are twelve pages in the main document, and twenty-six in the appendices, making thirty-eight in all,* but there is a peculiar pleasure in knowing the answer and slowly reconfirming it. *Like a miser recounting his money,* he thought, *the pure enjoyment of plenty. Going through the motions without any tension whatsoever. Like making love to someone one has known for years. No need for pretense, and no tension.* The dinner with Claire hadn't been a disaster at all, in spite of his worries. They both tried hard to spend the time together in a pleasant and civilized manner, and on overall they managed quite well. It was only after dinner that they didn't know what to do with themselves and it became somewhat awkward. She is very beautiful, although too skinny, he had observed.

The numbers are actually nicely printed in the top right corner of each page, which allows readers to resume where they left off on the page before, perhaps without even noticing the number. No disruption, no bumps, and no rough edges. Like knowing someone well. Don wonders whether all of these thoughts aren't attempts to convince him to return to Claire. "Messages from the unconscious," Irv would call them. He ponders the precise position of the numbers in the top right corner of each page and suddenly sees them as indicating one o'clock, a clear message that it is past noon. There is a potential danger in not noticing the numbers; days and years can pass by without awareness. One should be reminded of time. An entire lifetime can run so smoothly that by the time one notices, it is almost over!

Each appendix is labeled with a letter, and has its own numbers, starting from one. He realizes that this is not entirely consistent with the previous argument, since it definitely breaks the sequence. It epitomizes the idea of a fresh start, in contrast with the continuation of what came before. Is his relationship with Claire a direct continuation of their past together, or is it a fresh start? He reminds himself that an appendix is not independent of the main body of the report, and in many ways it's secondary to it. Don doesn't like this idea, and he thinks about what a strange word *appendix* is. The temptation to logovore it is clearly present, but he resists, and tries to acronym it instead but quickly gives up, knowing ahead of time that he will be unable to come up with something for the "x" at the end. How often can one use the word *xenophobia* anyway?

The report is neatly stacked and it is difficult to pick up just one page at a time. He hesitates to put pressure on the corners, something that he knows helps, so as not to damage the clean sheets. A page can be attached to the one preceding it and be easily missed. The same way an elephant can hide behind the body of the one standing next to it. Only by watching the herd closely for a long time can one be sure. With Claire too, only time will tell. Let her leave with Marion for Paris and give both of them time to think. *She insists on seeing me as a new person, which I'm not. The changes in her are also mostly superficial. If we were to go back living together it would certainly endanger the few personal developments that we might have managed to accomplish.* You cannot go back to an old relationship and hope that things will stay changed. In order for a change to work, it must be a long journey from which there is no way back.

His back still hurts. Last night, in the restaurant, when he made the wrong movement, he knew right away that it signaled at least one week of lower back pain. It was also an elegant solution to the question of how to end the evening. Even before he hurt himself he had noticed that the air conditioning was too cold, and that it meant trouble, but he was too embarrassed to ask to move to another table. He collects the report that has to be sent right away since it is already slightly overdue, and he reaches for the phone to call Dorothy. A sharp pain shoots across his back all the way down to his left thigh. Quickly he returns to his original position in his orthopedic chair, giving himself a rest. He knows that he will have to reach for the phone soon and plans his strategy. One way to accomplish the desired movement without undue pain would be to take hold of the table with both hands and pull the chair closer. It used to have small wheels, but he can't remember whether they are still there and doesn't want to move his neck to check. If successful, such a maneuver would bring his left hand within striking distance of the target. Another way would be to slowly stand up, both feet lifting his body at precisely the same time, and once up, push himself with his hands closer to the table, pull the phone toward him, and sit down. The advantage of this option is that it would solve the problem for all future phone calls today. He hates to think what would happen were the phone to ring right now, before he makes his preparations. Its main disadvantage is that if the chair does have wheels, he won't be able to push himself effectively, pushing the chair instead. He is still trying to feel out both options, to smell them out, when it occurs to him that this is what old age is like. He has just experienced the state of mind that is in store for him—the need for careful planning for even the slightest movement. He must tell Irv about it right away. The discovery that even negative experiences have the capacity for enriching one's existence is so exciting that without giving it another thought Don stands up and reaches for the phone.

www.ingramcontent.com/pod-product-compliance
Lightning Source LLC
Chambersburg PA
CBHW070006260626
47159CB00005B/1691